Someone's Late —
For a Very Important Date

"So, we're not doomed?"

Crosses laughed. "Far from it."

"And when Alice gets here— our savior and all that— will everything go back to the way it was?"

"Nothing ever goes back to the way it was," said Noughts. "And whether it becomes better or worse depends upon—"

"Me?" said Axford resignedly.

Noughts delicately placed the tips of her fingers together. "Not exactly."

"Oh," he said, and deflated.

"It depends in a large part upon the Alice herself."

"*The* Alice?"

"And upon the Queen, and upon your friend the raven, and upon Fred, and upon the rabbit—"

"Hold on, hold on, hold on," said Axford, throwing his hands up in the air, clearly suffering from information overload. "Who is Fred and who is the rabbit?"

A single slight frown crossed both identical faces, sliding from right to left without stopping.

"Sometimes the things unseen aren't entirely clear," Crosses said. "Apparently, someone named Fred is going to show up, someone unlike anyone ever seen in Wonderland before. And he's going to be important."

"Yes," agreed Noughts, "Fred is going to be very big when he gets here."

"And as for the rabbit— well, you'll find that out before too long. The Queen will show you."

Axford raised an eyebrow. "Oh, he's to do with the Queen, eh?"

"Well, he works for us, really—"

"But only the Queen can let him out of his cage."

He shook his head and sighed. "Do we have to feed him carrots?"

"*Dear* Axford," said the sisters through their peals of laughter. Even the giant cat snickered at him. "He's not *that* kind of rabbit."

Without Alice

A Novella More-or-Less of Wonderland

Random da Shea

ISBN-13: 978-0615701721
ISBN-10: 0615701728

Copyright Leeftail Press September 2012
www.leeftailpress.com

Chapter One

There was a sad little shop around the corner. It sat there dejectedly and did not move; the owner was worn out with crying and had taken himself off to bed.

The landscape around the empty shop was as pale and washed out as a water-color painting caught in the rain. If you traveled far enough west of the shop, you would eventually stumble upon a land made up of black and white squares: a giant's checkerboard. The black bled slowly into the white, like an approaching army encroaching on the borders of the next land over. Soon everything would be a nasty, indeterminate grey, like lint out of a dryer. If you went even further west, you'd reach a land where giant rabbit holes dotted the turf, large enough for a full-grown man to walk through with only stooping a little; the holes were collapsing slowly in on themselves, in the weight of the rain, like cakes with hollow middles.

It had been declared a national day of mourning— the entire countryside was as empty and barren as a house full of teenagers the morning after a late night.

The little shop sat quietly, silently, without noise, on its sad little foundation, much like a little shop sitting quietly, silently, and without noise, on its sad little foundation. It was small, it was silent, it was a light grey color, and there was a sign on the door.

It said, "Alice doesn't live here any more, either."

Nine years later, Axford Barrel sat with his legs swinging free. He rather liked doing that. He felt it emphasized the smallness of his stature, and he was correct.

"I don't know," he said in Cockney English to the dusty, peevish-looking raven who sat in front of Axford's perch, "everything's just gone to pot since Alice left."

The raven cocked its head at him. Axford's complaint was one it heard often, and still didn't understand. This was because it only spoke Raven English.

Axford heaved a sigh and shook his head, because he liked the heavy feel of his braided hair striking against his face. It gave him the sensation of weight, importance, style, a man about town instead of a town about man. The feel of things, in fact, was considerably more important to Axford than the reality. "Since Alice left," he said in Raven English, "everything's gone to pot."

He had to change the composition of the sentence because that was the way you spoke in Raven English. Ravens had one of the more sensible forms of language; there were actually creatures with whom, in order to communicate, you had to speak each word as though it were spelled backwards, and even some where you had to speak the words upside down. Axford had a fantastic head for languages, though, and he wasn't about to complain. "It could be worse," he was fond of saying, usually accompanying the phrase with a shrug. "After all, it could be that they had to use completely different words for each language; now, *that* would be difficult."

The raven opened his beak and clicked its tongue against it a few times, preparatory to speaking. "It could be worse," it said, with a shrug of his feathers. The raven spent rather too much time around Axford.

Axford pulled one of his braids forward. It was coming undone. He began doing it up again, well pleased as always with the dirty orangish color of the strands. His eyes were a dark ocean blue, sharks swimming in the depths. This, along with his hair, provided what he thought a very pleasing contrast to his pale skin. His eyebrows were orange, too, though he didn't know it.

All in all, he thought, capturing in his mind's eye the full effect of his small slim body and his orange corn-rows and his mildly curious face— all in all, while he looked the sort you might not trust to watch your children for more than ten minutes, he did not look the least bit like someone who might thieve you of your last shilling. Everything, then, was going according to plan.

"While you distract them," he said to the raven, after clicking his tongue against the roof of his mouth a few times, preparatory to speaking, "I will thieve them."

"Of their last shilling?" enquired the raven, after clicking its tongue against his beak, preparatory to speaking.

"Of their last shilling," agreed Axford, after clicking his tongue against the roof of his mouth. "While you distract them, you see. Of their last shilling, you see," he repeated, relishing the sound of his own voice. He did have rather a nice voice. It was light and fairly pleasant and decanted itself in the vaguely Celtic tones of his forefathers. It wasn't quite distinct enough to be conclusively defined as Irish, Scottish, or Welsh, as such labels did not exist in Wonderland— it was merely a touch of a lilt, just heavy enough to make his voice the embodiment of whimsical sound. He was very proud of it. "Though I prefer pound notes."

There were no more than a handful of shops here in the shadow of the Queen's Castle, but it was the main city in the country, the pride and joy of all the citizens. People traveled from all over to see it, with the end result that the few short streets were crammed continuously with a never-ending rush of people and animals and creatures, old groups fading out as new waves came in, a multi-faceted ocean of living, breathing, souvenir-buying beings.

Watching for a likely client two minutes ago, Axford Barrel had discovered that one of his chief pet peeves, heretofore unrealized, was people who licked their fingers preparatory to turning the pages of a book. It was distinctly unhygienic, he thought.

He'd discovered this while watching a man with rebellious hair (rebellious in that it was intent on falling out, which purpose the man was almost certainly not in concordance with) and a rebellious stomach (see above parentheses) who, as he read his book, licked his finger preparatory to turning a page.

"That's the man," said Axford to the raven, and then said it again so the raven could understand it.

The raven clicked its tongue against its beak. "Cadio just got him," he said, in Raven English.

"No!" said Axford. "Really? Curse Cadio anyway, the rat gizzard. It shows, doesn't it?"

The raven nodded for a moment, then gave up on pretending it knew what Axford meant by this. "What does?"

"Breeding." Axford sometimes forgot to say exactly what it was that he was thinking. "Cadio's mother was a Duchess, you know. No wonder we can't trust him."

The raven said nothing, wisely, but turned its head sideways and looked with no particular intent at a dust particle.

"I don't know," said Axford. "Everything's gone to pot since Alice left." And then he said it again, so the raven could understand it, which is where we came in.

Now, he turned his attention to the brick wall in front of which he was sitting. "What's that say?" he asked the raven, pointing to a mark on the wall.

The raven told him.

"Oh, my," said Axford. "That's rich. That's classic, that is."

"What?" said the raven, who could read but not comprehend Cockney English or its associated slang terms.

"When I talked like that around my mother," said Axford offhandedly, "she chopped me in two with a butcher knife." He pulled a quill pen stub from his pocket, licked it for fluency, and scrawled 'Turnips Forever' underneath the curse word some raven had marked on the wall. 'Turnips Forever' may not sound too radical to you, but it was quite a controversial remark to make in Cockney English.

"Let's do something, then," said Axford. Minor acts of graffiti always made him hungry.

"The prospect doesn't bother me unduly," said the raven.

Axford hopped down from his barrel and strode through the crowd. In fact, for the most part, he strode under the crowd— Axford was very small for his age, which was somewhere within shouting distance of thirty, or so. Approaching the beginning of his adolescent years, he had gotten tired at the very prospect of growing and simply stopped. He had not suffered by it.

The raven followed, hopping behind him and not looking to either side, with a single-mindedness that was usually found lacking in birds.

Axford found his way to the pub. There was only one other pub in the whole country, and it was too far away for him to get to, or he would have gone to it instead. This one sported arched doorways, yellowing paint, a framed comic painting of a fish emerging from a sort of underwater cocoon with bubbles coming from the fish's mouth, and a wry-faced bartender of indeterminate age and the female persuasion. Her name was Soul Train and she was particularly fond of Axford.

"I love your money," she said to Axford. "I believe you should give me double the usual amount, because I am in love with it. That is, if you want a drink."

"*I* don't want a drink," said Axford, hopping up on a stool and giving her a wide-eyed owl gaze. "I want soup, I'm hungry."

"What about you, Maverick?" said Soul Train in Cockney English, to the raven— the raven's name was Maverick, but since it was the only raven in that part of the country, it also answered to 'the raven,' 'blackbird,' and 'hey-you,' provided they were properly translated, of course.

"What?" asked the raven, semi-alertly. Axford rephrased the question so it could understand. "Ah. A small bowl of worms and a germ cocktail."

"Yuck," commented Soul Train, stepping back from the counter. This needed no translation. The raven chuckled.

"I'm kidding," it said. "I don't want the worms."

"What do you want?" asked Axford. "Soul Train's waiting."

"Soup!" said the raven enthusiastically. The raven spent rather too much time around Axford.

The truth about the soup was that it was 70% rice wine and quite a bit cheaper than a regular drink. Axford, when he thought about it, couldn't come up with a logical reason behind this. He subconsciously assumed it had something to do with a kind and benevolent Creator.

"Eight pence," said Soul Train, thumping the two bowls with the cold, pale reddish, watery soup down upon the counter. Axford held a finger up to tell her to wait, and looked around for a client.

There was a quiet-looking fellow sitting with his back to Axford, oblivious to everything around him. Always a promising beginning. Axford studied the cloth of his coat and found it promising as well: rich, thick, and well-cut. He slipped down from his stool and padded over to him.

The man merely sat there. He was definitely on the well-fed side, perhaps a bit too well-fed, if truth be told. His skin was well-sunned, with a slight olive cast to it that indicated recent illness or infrequent washing. He stared seriously into his drink. Wondering if it was safe, probably, which was a valid concern in this establishment. One minute he had a pocketbook and the next he didn't.

Axford took a sixpence out of it, delved deeper, found a pound note, grinned and put the sixpence back, then reconsidered and took both the sixpence *and* the pound note.

He tossed it at Soul Train, who, having watched the entire incident impassively, took the money without objection. She'd been in the pub business for a long time, and had no delusions about the honesty of her clientele. Axford was one of her better customers— he always paid his bill without fuss. Without his own money, either, but reliability outweighed such petty moral concerns. She knew that money was money was money, no matter who it came from. The point was that it ended up in her pocket.

Axford picked his bowl of soup up, his stomach making small noises of anticipation, and the raven buried his beak in his and gulped, lifting his head to swallow. They downed the thin liquid in a matter of seconds.

The raven almost drowned, but Soul Train reached over and plucked it out of the soup.

The bird panted and shook his feathers dry.

"Gotten more serious about its mission in life, has it?" he gasped, referring to the rice wine.

"I think so," said Axford, falling off his chair.

Through the haze that covered his eyes, he saw some police-shaped things come in the pub door. Perhaps they were, in fact, police, but his brain was by this point too fuzzed over to reach a conclusion. The only thing he could be sure of was that the man he'd taken the money from was now standing, quite slowly and seriously.

He turned round, and Axford wished heartily for the sweet oblivion of a sharp and sudden blow to the head.

It was Wolf. He'd thieved from Wolf.

The Queen's Wolf.

Chapter Two

Death came to Breca's parents, wearing a long black cloak, on a hot and sultry July Wednesday, just around twilight time.

"Good evening," he said, and bowed spectrally, if a little stiffly.

"Evening," said her dad, peering at him through the screen door.

"Nice weather," Death added.

"Mmm," said her momma suspiciously.

"I've come for your daughter," Death added.

"Pardon?" said her dad, who was as deaf as a post that had mislaid its hearing aid.

"Why?" demanded her mother. "She's only nineteen."

Death cocked his head. "Do you realize," he said, "I've never been asked that before."

"Really?" said her mother. "Why's that, do you think?"

"Well, I *am* death, you know," said Death. "I expect that must be it. When an impossibly tall, hooded black creature shows up at your door, it seems that you'd be rather more inclined to screaming than inviting him in for a philosophical conversation. Screaming, or playing chess. It's always one or the other."

"But why Breca?" persisted Breca's momma.

"Oh, that," said Death, flapping a skeletal hand. "I want to marry her."

"Pardon?" said her dad, for the reason previously stated.

"Yes," said Death, and added, "I want to take her away from all this."

"Don't be silly," said her momma. "You're death, you can't be married."

"Can't I?" said Death, mildly surprised.

"Of course not."

"I must admit to being mildly surprised," said Death, and added, "which is more than I've been in millennia. Why can't I be married?"

Breca's momma shrugged expressively, as though this was the most easily, obviously answered question that had ever been asked. "It's against the rules."

"What rules?"

"Those unspoken ones, the ones that everyone knows. Built in to us from the dawn of time."

"You just spoke it," Death objected, tilting his hood and whatever was inside it to one side in a quizzical manner.

"Unwritten, then."

Death seemed vaguely affronted. "You just show me where *that's* at. You think those apply to *me*?"

"Don't they?"

"Well, er— yes," said Death. There was a scraping noise as he shifted his weight uncomfortably. "I suppose it just bothers me to think that you humans know it. I mean, it's not very good for my dignity, is it. I'd rather you all think of me as something mysterious and unfathomable— and if that's the profile one is going for, one doesn't want people thinking one's got a lot of red tape one has to go through to get anything done. I mean, that's not very awe-inspiring, is it?"

"No," admitted Breca's mother, making a wry face at the floor. She'd dealt with a similar issue in her own professional life. Breca's momma was a conservative MP. "Still. That's the way it is. Sign of the times."

"I suppose," said Death doubtfully. "Well. So I'm not allowed to get married. Very well. I'll concentrate on getting that law changed later on, and for the present time we'll just be friends. Very special friends. Platonic," he added like an anxious boyfriend arriving to take his girl to the prom and trying to assure her parents as to his honorable intentions, none of which was far from the truth. "She's the most beautiful girl I've ever seen. And that's saying something. I've seen a few."

"Of course," said her momma, shifting pleasedly. " Takes after me, she does."

"Where is she?" Death enquired.

"In the tub."

Death traipsed his way to the bathroom and banged hollowly on the door.

"'Out in a minute," said Breca languidly.

"Out now," said Death.

"Who is it?"

"It is Death," said Death, and added, "come for **YOU**, Breca."

"Well, hold your spectral horses," said Breca. "I'm all soapy."

She rinsed, stepped out, dried off, swathed her body in a robe and her long red hair in a towel, and opened the door. Death, she reasoned philosophically, usually got what it wanted, though she did take a peek under his robe to make sure it wasn't just her boyfriend playing a joke. It wasn't. For one thing, she didn't have one, and for another, there was nothing under the robe but empty space, a blacker and denser darkness than she was used to even out here in the country of moonless nights.

"Come along, Breca," said Death, and, somehow, handlessly, took her by the hand.

"Can't I even say goodbye to my parents?"

"Wait until we're flying above your house on my pale horse."

"Why?"

"You sound like your mother," said Death, giving her a studious look. For the first time he began to doubt whether he was competent to handle whatever this was he was getting into. "Asking questions, needing to know why, stripping the romance from the unknown, bare-bonesing it, needing reasons and logistics. Everything, to you humans, is numbers. And then you change numbers back into letters again. I sat in on one of your college algebra lectures once—"

Breca gave him a questioning look.

"It's a long story," said Death, "or comparatively long anyway. My point is, I saw how things work for you. X + Why = B-cause. In this case, the answer is, *because* it's more dramatic that way." Breca had forgotten the question, and was prepared to say as much. "And besides," Death added, "I'm in a hurry."

He led her outside, her parents following behind in a desultory fashion, hangdog and bemused. Her mother lifted her hand to wave goodbye.

"Wait," Death commanded in stentorian tones. He put Breca on his horse, got up behind her, and gave the horse a nudge with his foot. The horse heaved a sigh. It was a very old horse. Carefully, as though its pale legs were made of glass, it took a few steps, then launched itself into the air.

"Quite a picture we must make," said Death into her hair. He heaved something like a gusty sigh. "Death, his pale horse, and," he added, "you."

"Yeah," agreed Breca. "Quite a picture."

She waved to her parents, who were by now looking quite tiny, and they waved back just before she lost sight of them. The horse circled higher, and she thought what a long way it would be to fall. Then the earth disappeared and she was surrounded by sky.

The raven woke up very slowly, in stages. His feet woke up first, then his left wing, followed by his right, the lower half of his body, the upper half, his head, and finally, his beak.

It opened. "Bloody turnips," it said.

"Yeah," agreed Axford who had been interestedly watching the raven's spasmodic twitching. "That's what I said when I woke up."

It must be noted that, if you should ever go to Wonderland, all mention of turnips must be avoided if you wish to remain in polite society. It is considered extremely rude and will be dealt with accordingly. One man who used the phrase "Turnips in a basket" while in the presence of Her Majesty the Red Queen Xylophone XIV was put on Death Row. But since nobody ever truly dies in Wonderland, the Queen relented and simply deprived him of the use of his body except for on alternate Wednesdays and Thursdays. An even more severe case was Death-In-The-Stocks, a well-known peace activist ('DITS' to his friends, of which he has few). During an audience with Her Majesty the White Queen A Minor, he unexpectedly blew up, and whilst carefully putting himself back together again, accused the Queen of unsubstantiated flipper-style turnipism. The Queen was profoundly shocked and, while a pacifist herself, ordered Death-In-The-Stocks to undergo Bach's Fifth Amendment Treatment, a specialty of the house. What remained of the imprudent peace advocate now spent all its time in a bottle.

Axford and the raven, however, had never been introduced to polite society and therefore had nothing to worry about.

The raven looked at his surroundings. "Bloody turnips," it said again.

"Yes," said Axford sympathetically. "I know."

"Turnip heaven in here."

"I said that, too."

They were in the Queen's dungeons. Axford had never been in them before (though he had once, as a child, taken a tour of the royal outhouses) but he knew that's what they were because there was a sign on the wall that said 'Welcome To The Queen's Dungeons!' in bright, sunny yellow letters. It had a map with a little red dot that said, cheerily, 'You Are Here.'

Axford scrutinized it, squinting closely to pick up any nuances of line or shape, but it didn't help. "A fat lot of good this does us," he said, unhappily. "The exits aren't marked."

"I don't think," said the raven, speaking slowly and sticking its tongue out a lot to test the air, "that we're meant to get out of here on our own."

"What?" said Axford. "You think they're going to help us?"

The raven glared at him.

"Oh, you'll get out of here all right," said a soft, spooky voice from the corner. "Though probably not all in one piece."

"You may even," said a slightly more raucous voice, "leave a few pieces behind."

Out of the shadows emerged a frightening nightmare, looming with a loominess that verged on the fantastic. Electric-green eyes glowed in the darkness. Primal white teeth bared themselves. Light glinted along the edge of the double-headed axe it carried. It strode up to Axford and tapped him on the knee.

Axford looked down at the gnome and resisted the impulse to flatten himself on the ground so he could gaze into its eyes. Gnomes don't like to be condescended to, and at the slightest hint will attack— the axe may not have been very big, but it was clearly razor-sharp, and Axford's legs were perfectly acceptable targets.

"Look here, my good dwarf," said the gnome in a husky, sweet voice, like old brandy. "Be a friend and lift me to the water trough."

"I'm not a dwarf," said Axford automatically, leaning down and extending a hand for the gnome to climb onto.

"Aren't you, by Her Majesty," said the gnome. He tapped Axford's chin in passing as Axford lifted him to the trough. "Thought it was a bit odd, never seen a dwarf without a beard before."

He knelt on the rim of the trough and scooped water in his hands, then drank quite slowly. When he was done he ran his hands over his face and sat on the rim, swinging his legs.

"I am Cheesebread," he announced.

There came a clatter from the corner he had recently vacated, as if someone had dropped a wooden bowl.

"And the one who just dropped his wooden bowl over there in the corner," Cheesebread went on, waving a hand in that direction, "is Dap-Hodil."

"Who or what is Dap-Hodil?" asked the raven.

"I'm not entirely sure," said the gnome with a slight frown. "People usually have their own opinions on the subject. Dap-Hodil! Come! Show yourself! They promise not to laugh, don't you?" he asked Axford and the raven. They both agreed hurriedly. "See, they promise not to laugh," repeated the gnome, and then whispered out of the side of his mouth, "He's going to hold you to that, you know."

Axford had time for one startled glance at him before the shadows moved into the light and took on form.

In the silence that followed as Axford and the raven stared in shock and Cheesebread in a kind of misplaced pride, the thing that was called Dap-Hodil dropped its wooden bowl again.

"I'm sorry," it said, revealing itself as the owner of the slightly-more-raucous-than-Cheesebread's voice. "I'm a bit accident prone."

Dap-Hodil was nine feet tall, his head near the top of the ceiling. His form was somewhere between species— too leanly muscular to be entirely human, not hairy enough to be entirely lupine. Besides which, he walked on his hind legs, leaning forward, with his shoulders hunched like an adolescent boy who'd recently undergone a growth spurt he wasn't entirely comfortable with. His eyes were silver in the shadows, and the hair that fell over them was thick and black and brushed his shoulders.

"Oh," said Axford, who had only recently retrieved his tongue from the back of his throat, where it had gone to hide when he tried to swallow his tonsils. He didn't feel particularly like laughing. "You're one of those."

"It's a problem," said Dap-Hodil, looking down at the two halves of the wooden bowl it held, and trying to fit them back together again. "Because, see, when I drop things— from my height— it tends to do so much more damage, you see. This is the fifth bowl I've been through."

"And," Cheesebread added, veritably bursting with pride over his cellmate, "he's only been here two weeks. How's that for quick work?"

"Very nice," said Axford, reckoning it in his best interest that he be complimentary. "Can you tell me something of the procedure around here?"

Cheesebread and Dap-Hodil exchanged glances. It was a bit of a stretch for both of them.

"Well," began Cheesebread, tapping his fingers together pensively, "you're brought here to the dungeons, landed with a sentence the length of which varies according to your crime, and imprisoned for however long is deemed appropriate. You're given food and water every day, and you have to entertain yourself." He paused. "Some folks don't seem to handle that too well."

"What happens to them?" asked the raven, while not entirely sure it wanted to know.

"They end up crap-shooting with their mental marbles— and subsequently losing their shirt. Psychologically, of course."

"How nice," said the raven sadly. The raven was an intelligent bird, and it knew that to be confined with no flying room was invariably the end of all intelligent birds.

"That won't happen to us, though," said Cheesebread cheerfully.

"Why not?"

"We're serious offenders here. We repeat, recall, recommit. We're on Death Row."

"Death Row?" asked Axford, and despite the general look of things had to smother an incredulous laugh. "There's no death in Wonderland. How can it have its very own row?"

"An apt point," conceded the gnome. "I guess they'll just have to do something horrible to us instead."

Breca cast a glance downwards. Clouds covered the earth, except for occasional glimpses of what looked like mountains. Every once in a while she caught the glimmer of refracted light, reflecting from some far-off water. She tapped Death's bony shoulder.

"Is this as fast as he goes?" she shouted above the wind.

"Of course not." Death's voice, deep and old, carried— he had no need to shout. It was one of those perks you get when you're death, along with access to the best restaurants and fresh flowers in your room every morning.

"Then why aren't you going faster?"

"Believe me, if he was going as fast as possible, you wouldn't like it."

Breca pondered this in silence for a bit. "So where are we going then?"

"I'm going to drop you off home, if you don't mind. Sheol, that is." He sounded just a tad embarrassed. "I did try to sweep up, but I've been pressed for time, so please ignore the mess."

"What?" she shouted. Then— "Is that anywhere close to Glasgow? I've got family in Glasgow that I wouldn't mind—"

"You can stay there while I make my rounds. Sheol, not Glasgow, I mean. You won't be lonely— there's lots of souls there. They're not much for conversation, but they *are* there. And," he added, "I'll be home for dinner every couple hundred years."

Breca, full up to the brim with horror, committed a desperate act. She jumped, or rather fell on purpose, off the horse.

She hovered for a second on a particularly strong updraft, then began the fall towards earth. Behind her, above her, she could hear Death yell something not fully comprehensible, but somewhere along the lines of, "I'll come after you!"

She was terribly afraid he would.

Chapter Three

The Queen was brushing the green streaks from her yellow hair. She didn't know why— at least, while she had her suspicions, she wasn't absolutely sure— but every morning since she had been crowned, she'd awoken with green streaks snaking their way from the ends of her hair upwards to her scalp. The mornings when she woke late, the green streaks had nearly reached the roots. On those days it took her longer to get rid of them, and she attacked her hair ferociously with the brush.

Now, she brushed the last one into oblivion and surveyed the effect in the mirror. Perfect. There was practically no more to be done. She leaned closer to the mirror, reached up and adjusted her crown a little. She didn't like being without the crown. She ate in it, bathed in it, swam in it. Sometimes she even slept in it, despite the headache that inevitably followed the next morning.

With an absent hand as she watched her reflection, she reached out to her dogs, who snarled and whined in a keening litany, flinching away from her touch. The spikes that poked through their collars and latched into their skin held them close against the wall, but they were frail protection against the havoc they could wreak if they got loose. The dogs were both more and less than ordinary pets: Wonderland's most perfect fighting machines, true, but difficult to play fetch with as the object thrown would be annihilated far before it ever reached you again.

She called for her servant, Widden. "Widden!" she said.

He came to her, as silent as ever, his hair tousled and his teeth freshly brushed. He'd been her manservant since she took the throne, and long familiarity had indeed bred contempt, however carefully hidden.

"Up early this morning, Your Majesty," he remarked. "Fine bright day."

It was raining. The Queen said as much.

"It's raining, Widden," she said.

"Your Majesty is correct," said Widden, peering out the window. "It is raining."

"It's always raining." She sniffed. Rain didn't bother her. "What's for breakfast?"

"As Your Majesty is still on a diet, half a stick of celery and a grapefruit."

"Anything that isn't green or pink?"

"Coffee, Your Majesty. It's black," he added helpfully.

The Queen's look of utter revulsion was a daily sight Widden had come to look forward to. The lips wrinkled back, baring slightly bluish teeth, the eyes spit-fired, the brow furrowed savagely till you could plant corn in it if you were of a horticultural frame of mind. It did not last long, but Widden enjoyed it while it did.

"Never mind that," she said. "Peanut butter, for the celery? Sugar, for the grapefruit?"

"No chance of either, milady," said Widden cheerfully. "When you put on half a pound two weeks ago and had one of your, er, turns, Cook threw everything out except celery, grapefruit, and water crackers."

"Why in Wonderland—" started the Queen.

"Because you'd told her to, in no uncertain terms," said Widden accommodatingly, out of kindness to the cook. "And so, not only is there just celery and grapefruit to eat— it's also been there two weeks."

"I want a new cook," said the Queen, and got dangerous.

Breca was still falling.

She fell down, down, down.

This, she thought, must be what Alice felt when she fell down the rabbit-hole— falling forever. She tried a curtsey, curiously, reckoning she would never get the chance again. At least she hoped she wouldn't. At any rate, she was almost immediately unsuccessful as the wind caught at her robe and tried to get it away from her. She engaged in a prolonged tug-of-war, which finally she won at the expense of her fingernails. She'd lost the towel from her hair long ago, which she regretted, as towels were extremely useful things to have around.

She fell farther.

She fell farther than that.

She fell farther than that.

She landed.

She sat up. She wasn't dead. "How did that happen?" she wondered, and remembered that death was currently flying high above her, undoubtedly distracted. She wasn't even hurt. She was just very, very, very, very shaken.

Luckily, she had landed right next to a pub.

A jailer came to visit. He was handsome and cheerful and quite insane, because to do the sort of job he had, you have to be a bit unhinged anyway, or it'd drive you crazy. It wasn't just the isolation, it was the long hours. When he'd first gotten the job, he'd been no more than slightly unbalanced. That hadn't lasted long. Surrounded as he was by people who were desperately clinging to the shreds of their sanity with varying degrees of success, he simply gave up and went mad. He had now progressed to the point where the thought of spending a week in his room, accompanied only by one of those games where you have to get the ball into the little hole, thrilled him.

"Hullo," he said cheerfully.

"How are you," he said cheerfully, leaping nimbly to a separate paragraph.

"I'm your friendly neighborhood jailer," he said cheerfully, leaping again, and giggled. "This is going to sound funny, but walrus pants."

"Lovely to meet you, Mister Jailer, sir," said Axford, gripping the bars of the cell. He didn't mind crazy. He was well acquainted with it. "Ah, when might we get out, sir?"

"Oh, you're serving time for a bit more," said the jailer cheerfully.

"How much is a bit?"

"Quite a bit, a bit is," the jailer said cheerfully, after thinking this over for a while.

"I see."

"Yes indeed. Anyway, quite nice in here, don't you find? No worries."

"No?"

"Of course not. What kind of jail do you think this is?" The jailer harrumphed, cheerfully indignant.

"No, for instance, torture?" pressed Axford.

The jailer paused a moment and looked down at him in surprise. "Oh yes, well, we have that. We do the odd spot of torture now and then, occasionally. On occasion, as it were. Yes. No problem there. Torture? Lovely stuff. We've got professionals, you know. They get announced once a week, and the best one gets a plaque and an 'Employee of the Month' badge. Sorry, did I say a plaque? I meant plague. Gets the plague. And, of course, occasionally the Queen herself condescends to wield the whip. Though that's usually reserved for special occasions. Her birthday, for instance."

"And there's no chance of getting out anytime soon?"

The jailer stood and nodded stupidly at him for the several seconds it took before the question reached his brain, and then he said, "Oh, no, none at all. Why would you *want* to? Such a lovely place in here on occasion, such a lovely lovely place on occasion, such a lovely lovely lovely lovely—"

Axford looked at the raven. The raven shrugged its feathers at him and looked at Cheesebread. Cheeesebread didn't do much of anything because he was staring at the still-babbling jailer with morbid fascination, tiny mouth slightly agape.

"Of course," said the jailer suddenly, interrupting himself and looking surprised at his own audacity, "you could always take the way the Queen suggests."

"And that would be?" prompted Axford.

"Co-operation."

"With what?"

The jailer became quite agitated by this question and stared at the floor, the ceiling, and the walls for about two minutes each, muttering to himself about horticulture. Finally he said, "I don't know, you'd better ask the Queen." He smiled frantically, but not with his mouth.

"But we're in a jail," Axford reminded him patiently. "We can't get to the Queen."

"Not unless you've got an appointment," agreed the jailer.

"And have we got an appointment?"

"Yes. Thanks *so* much for reminding me. Come on, let's go, we're late."

If not for the fact that Axford, at this time of life, was far past being surprised, this would have surprised him. As it was, he simply blinked and said, "Well, let us out then."

"Right-o," said the jailer cheerfully, and put the key in the lock. "Oh, first, d'you mind locking your ankles up in those chains over there? The Queen likes a bit of security now and then—"

The manacles were standard-man size, which would have been fine, had there been any standard men around to use them. They wouldn't fit around Dap-Hodil's ankles, and the others simply stepped out of them the first time they attempted to move.

"Ah well. At least we can say we tried, hey? Never mind that," said the jailer. He opened the door. "Step this way, join the others."

"Others?" said Axford.

Standing in the corridor outside the cell were several beings of multiple origins and backgrounds. There was another gnome, slightly larger and much seedier than Cheesebread, two yellow-furred Chimeras, eyeing each other distrustfully, two Fiendish Thingies, a gaarden spider (800 times the size of your ordinary garden-with-one-

A spider) several beings who looked vaguely like humans but were in fact, if you cared to delve into their lineage, not entirely so, though of course no one in their right mind would delve into their lineage, not unless they had nothing in particular else to do that year. Along with these were another, smaller Fiendish Thingie, who looked quite uncomfortable at being by itself, a giant chicken or three, a centaur, and a Carpenter.

Axford and his companions stepped into line. They were directly behind the Carpenter, and quite passionately wished they weren't, for he was mumbling to himself and rattling his chains like a ghost.

"Here we go!" said the jailer, cheerfully. "Start up! Sound off!"

Sounding off, in this case, sounded like this:

"One!"

"Two!"

"Three!"

"Um!" (Frantically.)

"Six?" (Unsurely.)

"Six." (Confidently.)

"Forty-two."

"Eleven— I think—"

"Grrr."

(Confused silence.)

(Giggle)

"Fifteen."

(Confused silence.)

"Ten and nine!" (The raven.)

"Twenty-eight!" (Axford.)

"Ow!" (Cheesebread, who'd just been stepped on by Dap-Hodil.)

"Oops, sorry." (Dap-Hodil.)

This sad state of affairs being immediately due to the fact that very few of them could count higher than three. Not, at least, fast enough to fill present requirements.

The jailer remarked, "Well, that's the public school system for you. Shall we try it again?"

This suggestion was greeted by a chorus of groans.

"Oh, come now, come now," said the jailer. "I've never heard such a lack of enthusiasm. What will the Queen think? I shudder to speculate." And he did shudder, quite violently, getting speculation all over the floor.

They tramped on, each busy thinking of what, exactly, the Queen would think when she saw them— or, more importantly, what she would say. They knew there was no death in Wonderland, but there'd been rumors spread about that Her Majesty was trying to arrange for him to visit. There was, underneath the clinking of chains, and the shuffle of feet, or whatever passed for feet, a very worrying silence, the kind that suggested that the walls, floors, and ceilings were all keeping dirty secrets that had to do with certain high-ranking government officials.

"This place—" said Axford to the raven.

"Yes," said the raven, who had a feeling where he was going with this.

"This place knows something we don't know."

"And it ain't telling," said the raven emphatically.

"I'm rather glad of that. I don't like it as it is, silent. It'd be that much worse if it were speaking."

They walked on, passing through several doors that the jailer had to unlock, let them through, and then lock again, all of which was about as much fun as, and more tedious than, a traffic jam.

"I suppose we should feel flattered," said Axford. "They thought we were dangerous enough to put us behind all these locked doors."

"Dangerous has nothing to do with it," said Cheesebread, marching along double-quicktime to keep his place in line. "It's just that the Queen didn't much like the look of any of us."

"Really?"

"Really. That's how she decides who or what goes where for how long. All the good-looking fellows are let free, or, at least, kept closer to her quarters."

Axford was appalled. "But I've got such nice hair," he said.

"Ah, well, then undoubtedly in your case it was sheer jealousy."

"I'm quite serious, Cheesebread. How could she not take pity on my hair? Has she no heart at all?"

"Weren't you paying attention during your trial?"

"I had a trial?"

"You weren't, then."

Axford felt compelled to explain. "No, see, they had knocked me out. The last thing I remember is— she gave me some bad soup— and this man with empty pockets got up—"

"Oh, that," said Cheesebread dismissively. "They do that occasionally if there doesn't seem to be any other way of getting their man. It's a cheap trick really. Let me guess— it was Soul Train, wasn't it?"

"Again," said Axford, quite pleased by this, "rather flattering, don't you think? They had no other way of getting their man— I was just too wily and foxy-clever for them by half, now, wasn't I?"

"Of course, I heard a rumor— just a rumor— that in your case it was just that Wolf didn't like you much."

"Oh."

"Could be completely *unfounded* rumor."

"Could be."

Axford sent a series of suspicious glances at the doors and corridors as they passed through them.

The jailer dropped back and said to Axford, "No need to be

worried, son, the Queen's not really *that* keen on torture. Not on doing it herself, anyway. Blood is hard to get out of your royal robes. Though she does like to watch whenever possible."

"I'm not worried," said Axford. This was a blatant lie.

"No, but you're terribly tense, though."

"Not at all. Not tense. Not tense. I'm *alert*, if that's what you mean. Ready, you know."

The jailer considered this. "What are you ready for?"

"Anything," said Axford. He sensed something out of the corner of his ear, and he swung and focused on it.

"What's the matter?"

"Nothing— only— that wall."

The jailer looked at it. It looked like a perfectly ordinary wall to him.

"It looks like a perfectly ordinary wall to me," he said. He tried squinting from different angles but the only effect this had was to make him dizzy, so he stopped. "Why, what's wrong with it?"

"Nothing wrong. Nothing wrong with it, it just giggled at me is all."

"How nice," said the jailer, delighted, because here was a prisoner who had, obviously, the same type personality the jailer had: specifically, the sort that was most likely to be found deep in theological discussions with coconuts and other inanimate objects. Walls were an acceptable substitute.

"You have many giggling walls in this vicinity, do you?"

"No— not till recently. At least, not that I've noticed. I may have been *imagining* that they're not speaking, but—"

Axford swung round suddenly, nearly losing his balance on the slippery floors, and nailed a wayward partition with his steely gaze.

Looks like a mad pygmy, thought the jailer. *Pity about his hair.*

"Funny," Axford remarked, "there seem to be a lot of them now."

"Oh well," said the jailer, "this castle knows an awful lot more than it lets on."

"Does it?" said Axford, glaring at the floor and treading extra heavily.

The jailer ran on to open another door for them, and they found themselves in the throne room.

"Best behavior," he admonished each one as they walked past him. "No telling where this audience might go if you play your cards right. And that's actual cards, not just some racist agenda against the Queen's soldiers." He waited till they'd all filed past, then skirted inside behind them and closed the door, carefully, and shut tight.

Breca pulled herself up over the bar with the profound sensation that somehow, somewhere, there were other worlds; worlds in which she was not sure where or what or why she was. Worlds in which even her internal monologue made sense. Worlds spun by improbable words, and even more improbable authors. Probably the author was tired, so tired her eyes were watering, and her vision blurring and her pen dropping from her hand—

Latent panic was more potent than anything the bartender was offering at the moment.

Oh, to Whom It May Concern, Breca thought blurrily, *protect me from late-night philosophers, early-afternoon couch potatoes, and impoverished artistes.*

And Death, of course.

The Queen was quite a sight. Had Axford been good with words, he probably would have described her as a chill white something-or other, with her golden hair shining like seaweed, golden seaweed.

Axford was not good with words. He thought the Queen had the hair of a yak, the eyes of a wasp, and the heart of a rabbit, though admittedly not your ordinary rabbit. Although even ordinary rabbits will turn and fight and make squeaking noises, they only occasionally do all this and throw things, including, in this case, the Queen's Chief Advisor.

"She's in a fine mood today," whispered the jailer jovially as the unfortunate Chief Advisor landed on all four feet and scuttled sideways out of the room, chased by the Queen's large and terrifying black dogs, which snapped at his back with vicious intent. "How's *that* for regality?"

"Is she often like this?" muttered Axford back.

"Oh, no, often much worse. Threw the whole throne last time," the jailer said. Axford did not find this to be particularly reassuring.

The raven, as a matter of fact, was the only one of the convicts not shaking with fear. As a bird, it knew what it was to be soaring oh-so-many feet above earth, to catch a warm updraft that speaks to you of Brazil, or somewhere else where they grow lots of nuts, to float divinely along it, and then lose half your feathers in a freak cold front that creates a whirlwind before you can say Polly-want-a-cracker. This Queen with her flashing eyes and heaving shoulders and yellowed hair and ivory hands and buck teeth and chill whiteness *moved* him.

The raven became painfully aware that it was staring, beak open, at Its Majesty the Queen. It developed a sudden, intense interest in its left claw. Underneath its feathers, it was blushing.

It wasn't that the Queen was actually all that pretty— but she'd heard of places in which lack of body fat was the epitome of perfection. The Queen liked that idea. Skinny she could do. Skinny was a reachable goal. As far as skinny went, the Queen had it made.

"She's quite— thin," croaked the raven.

"It's the extent of her appeal," admitted Axford.

"Perhaps it's her firm conviction that she's beautiful that makes people admire and complement her so," said the jailer, tipping his head to one side. "Perhaps that's it. Sheer force of personality. You can say that if you like. Though, I think, if you were to assume that it was because she was the most powerful being in the country, you'd be more accurate."

Whatever it was, the raven appreciated it. It *liked* it. *Come a revolution*, it thought, *I will definitely* not *be the first to join.*

The Queen turned to look at them and they all stood up straighter. She stared for a few minutes and then began to curl her lip, slow and sure as a tidal wave.

It was quite a look, and quite a pity Widden wasn't there to see it, for he would have enjoyed it. But the Queen had discovered that he kept a small blue hamster under his bed as a pet and sent him to the stocks for being unmanly.

When she was done curling her lip and had, with a few moments of worry, got it straight again, she said languidly, "Hullo." Her voice was nothing to write home about, but it rolled over the raven like a thick dark tide of chocolate, completing its inter-species discombobulation. It fainted.

Axford nudged it carelessly with his foot till the raven's eyes opened.

"Get up," he hissed. "She's going to speak."

"I'll stay where I am, then," hissed the raven back, quietly, through its beak. "I couldn't possibly take it."

The Queen had taken notice of all this and was glaring at them. Axford gave her a nervous grin, kicked the raven again to no effect, and subsided.

"Gentle creatures," spat the Queen, still glaring, "considering you're on Death Row, I should think you'd be very grateful for the opportunity I am about to give you."

One by one, the prisoners caught and held their respective breaths. The tension was palpable. It made Axford seasick.

"And even if you aren't, it's not like you've got a whole lot of choice. But I want you to feel privileged anyway. And if you don't, you will answer to me." This was less than reassuring. The Queen rocked back on her heels and snapped her hands together behind her back and *glared*. "Now, I always thought of Wonderland as a terrific place. It's been brought to my attention recently, however, that there is one crucial element which it lacks."

A few of the prisoners were forced to breathe at this point. They didn't particularly want to, but there was only so long they could hold out.

The Queen stood solidly and, with typical regality, managed to look each and every one of them in the face.

"I want you all to go and look for Alice," she said, imperiously.

"I've been thinking," said the jailer conversationally to the guard, who stood at strict and rather painful attention by him. Standing at attention in Wonderland involves precariously high heels and rather a lot of needles.

"Oh no, not again," was what the guard said.

"Oh yes. I know the doctor said it wasn't good for me in my condition, but that was just at first, and I've gotten over that bad patch and consider myself a much happier, if less sane, man."

"It may not be very good for you," said the guard. "But it's terrible for the rest of us. Why didn't you submit to that lobotomy like your mother told you to?"

"I've *explained* it to you. The doctor kept washing his hands. Nobody's going to get soap in *my* brain. No *sir*."

"Doctors are *supposed* to wash their hands," moaned the guard, lifting his chin a little higher. He'd been over this before.

"*And* he was eating a pastrami sandwich—"

The jailer was quite happily off on a tangent, if indeed you could used the word 'tangent' without being redundant, in applying it to a man whose entire thought process had more meanders in it than a twenty-foot boa constrictor. What he'd started out to say was, he'd been thinking that when the Queen had made her suggestion, the prisoners had looked at her exactly as though she'd just laid an egg.

Chapter Four

They'd been given a unique opportunity: the chance to go and see the people who were behind all the major decisions made in Wonderland. Behind quite a few of the smaller ones, too, because you couldn't be too sure, ever, that what you decide to have for dinner isn't going to change someone's life forever. The decision between salad and a hamburger, if nothing else, certainly made a difference to the cows, and to the lettuce if it comes to that.

The Queen didn't put it quite this way, of course. She said, rather, that they were going to visit some relics from the past. She said this because she was the Queen and, like many who crave positions of power and know the position belongs to someone else, tried to downplay the ability of her superiors. It wasn't generally known that there were others in a higher position than her, because she did such a good job of being a public figurehead of authority. And after all, when people had questions about who owned which house, whose child was whose, who had the right of way when it was a four-way stop and there was a donkey in the middle of the street and Mercury was in the rising, they went to the Queen. They did not go to two tall, cool girls of several hundred years of age each, who sat eternally in steel-lined silver chairs and watched with quiet eyes everything that went on. Everywhere.

There were several Queens, of course. And numerous Kings. And many assorted Duchesses, Dukes, Princes, Princesses, and noblemen in Positions of Authority in their Particular Provence. But there were only two Noughts and Crosses. One Noughts and one Crosses, that is: one of each.

The convicts were shown into the Room one at a time. The Carpenter went in first and came out crying. No-one seemed to be able to muster much sympathy for him.

The larger chimera went in next, and while he was inside, Axford and the raven looked about them. They sat in very smooth, comfortable chairs that, with a little shoving, could be made to fit the shape of each creature. It was a long, low room, which connected to a long, low corridor which sloped gently downward for a long, low time from where they had entered it from the kitchen pantry. Very few people knew the passage was there. The number had increased significantly now, and this made Axford rather nervous. If they were inclined to take the numbers down again, how long would Axford's life be worth anything?

Not long.

Not low, either.

Axford didn't much care for the thoughts he was thinking. He shifted uncomfortably in his marvelous chair, put his elbow on the armrest and turned his face into his hand, trying to hide behind it.

"Nervous," said the soft voice to his left. It was not a question.

"Mmph."

"Why?"

"Mmph," said Axford, with slightly more conviction.

"You're thinking maybe we're not in the safest position. A secret's not a secret when half the prison's in on it."

Axford picked his head out of his hands and looked at the voice. It belonged to the Fiendish Thingie who was on his own. Axford thought how peculiar it seemed— he'd never seen a lone Fiendish, as they were paired up at birth and were never meant to be without a companion. This in itself was enough to intrigue Axford— but then he took a good look at the Fiendish's face, and stopped still.

All Fiendishes have a specific set of characteristics: six fingers on the left hand, an otherwise quite normal humanoid body from the shoulders down, a dark ring around their neck like certain types of ducks, silver eyes, long blond hair, large diamond-shaped ears that reach past the outlines of their skulls, and snouts like huge noses that start between their eyes and slant far out, then slant back in just in time for their lower lip to meet up with it. They're very difficult to kiss for this reason. They also lack nostrils, and breathe instead through their ears.

This lone Fiendish Thingie had all those things— except his eyes were brown, and his hair dark, dark far beyond black.

"You're all alone," said Axford.

The Fiendish dropped his head a tiny bit in acknowledgment.

"Why?"

The Fiendish licked his lip. His strange eyes never left Axford's. "She's gone," he said. "She couldn't take the dungeons, and she went mad. They moved her somewhere else after that. I don't know where."

"How long have you been down there?" Axford asked, appalled.

"Too long," whispered the Fiendish after a bit. One of his dark eyes twitched rapidly, and he put one hand up to cover it, pressing all six fingers against it.

Axford shifted his gaze to the floor, and fidgeted in a fairly useless manner, attempting to disguise his discomfort by playing an imaginary flute for a moment. "I'm Axford Barrel," he offered.

The Fiendish turned a one-eyed look on him, still holding the other with his hand. "You're not a dwarf."

"No."

"My name is Eldritch Rune. Her name is Gibbous." The past tense seemed to escape him. He probably hadn't had much occasion to use it.

"Uhn?" said Axford. He could have said, "Really?" in the exact same tone but he didn't wish to sound incredulous.

"We're going to be sent away," whispered the Fiendish to his lap. "Probably we won't be returning."

Axford couldn't help wishing he didn't take such a pessimistic view of things, but he got the feeling that the Fiendish's conversation wasn't, strictly speaking, directed at him. The Fiendish's next words more or less confirmed this.

"Who cares," is what he said next. "It doesn't matter."

Axford shook his head at him. "Matters to *me*," he said.

"Why?"

"Well—"

"Why?" Rune repeated, his eyes intense. "What've you got to live for— *who've* you got to live for?"

This was a question Axford had never asked himself— he had in fact taken great pains to avoid doing so. And now, confronted with it unexpectedly, he wasn't sure what to say. He couldn't very well say 'the raven,' as that particular bird was busy living for itself.

"Well, me, I guess," he said finally.

"And that's enough for you?" pressed Eldritch Rune.

'Yes." Axford didn't feel he could say anything else at this point, not without breaking down in tears because no-one loved him. He shifted in his seat, frowned slightly to himself, and swallowed hard. The Fiendish Thingie stared at him for a minute then looked at the floor.

"I see," he remarked in a tiny voice, though he probably didn't see at all.

The door opened and the chimera stumbled out. He did not look keen. He looked about as unkeen as an unwhetted banana. If you tried to cut through a wall with the banana and, as is almost inevitable, ended up smashing it to bits and embedding it in the wallpaper, the remains would be a fairly accurate representation of what the chimera looked like at this point. He sank into his chair as his hand came loose from his arm in a long sticky goo; with moody intent he leaned over, picked it up, and settled to sticking it back on. The two Fiendish Thingies went in next, holding tightly onto one another's hands.

Axford watched them go.

Then he turned to Rune and said, "If you found someone else, would you be happy?"

"Someone else?" said Rune, as if he'd never before heard the words.

"Yeah, someone other than—" Axford having got this far, suddenly realized that he didn't know the polite term for a Fiendish's ex-partner, probably because there'd never been cause to invent one. He blindly hazarded a phrase in Raven English— "before now the one you had"— and hoped for the best. "You know, Gibbous."

Rune looked mortally offended for a minute, but Axford had been pretty much resigned to that happening anyway. He sighed and turned away to rest his chin on his hand.

But then Rune sat looking down at his empty hands and said, "Yes, I believe I could," in bewildered tones.

Axford turned back and gave him a relieved grin.

"But it'd be difficult to find someone— after all, no-one else is in my situation."

"Why is your hair dark and your eyes not silver?" demanded the raven abruptly. He'd been eavesdropping eagerly in case the conversation turned to debating the Queen, and now found curiosity to be a bit too much for him.

Axford jumped when the raven spoke, having gotten rather deeper in the conversation than he'd intended, but the Fiendish, not startled at all, said, "My grandmother on my father's side was a—" and stopped as a sudden thought struck him painfully atop the head and arrested him in mid-sentence. Or, if not precisely mid-, then well into the final third.

Axford watched his eyes widen and his mouth open slightly in surprise. For a moment he looked quite like a bird.

"What's that mean, she was 'A'?" demanded the raven waspishly.

"Yes after all why not why shouldn't I be able to *he* did it," was what tumbled out of Rune's mouth a minute later.

"Ah," said Axford. "Your grandmother was human?"

"Yes—"

"Ohhh," said the raven. "One of those."

"What happened to the first— Mrs. Rune's Grandmother?" He found himself again without a polite term.

"I don't know. But— I do know that my grandfather met my grandmother shortly after he was picked up for assaulting a dummy."

Axford was surprised. "Ventriloquism-related violence? That hardly seems an arresting offense."

Rune looked puzzled. "No. They were playing bridge. He got quite upset."

"Ah."

The door opened. The raven was next, and it hopped from its seat carelessly.

"Are you not worried?" asked Axford.

"I'm a bird," said the raven. "What are they going to do to me?"

It went in. Axford exchanged glances with Cheesebread.

It came out; some of its feathers seemed to be missing.

"They want you," it gurgled to Axford, and fell asleep in its chair.

With considerable trepidation, Axford stepped down from his seat and approached the door, which was ajar about half a foot. He slid through it and it closed behind him— those outside heard it clang, but inside all noise was muffled. Axford had to check his pulse to make sure his heart was still beating.

It was not an impressively large room. It was painted a shade of off-white, which gave it a sort of gentle ivory glow. There were two people in it. There was nothing else to look at.

Axford stood and stared.

They were identical in every way (pale-skinned and dark eyed and slightly-lavender hair and peaceful faces) except above one's head hovered like a halo a luminous circle and above the other, a luminous x. On Crosses' lap sat a large calico cat with curiously alert eyes and prominent teeth.

They sang a tune that echoed in his mind as vaguely familiar, though he couldn't place it for the life of him.

"Watch the sun die, we are all dying
"We've nowhere to go to, nowhere to run
"We hold to each other and hope that by lying
"We can keep living, outliving the sun.

"Dance it away, sing the song of deception
"Illness, disease, shattered heart, broken bone
"Old age and anger, can't face tomorrow
"Lose yourself in the song of the lost and alone

"It's only us now, and we sing a lament
"There was no such thing as the one and only
"Days draw to a close, what's won is spent
"This beautiful ghost of the lost and the lonely"

They watched him staring as the song drew to a close, and slow smiles crept across their faces.

"How very *interesting*, sister," said one.

"Very," agreed the other. They did not embellish and the smiles were silent substitutes for laughs.

Axford was not too stunned to be unaware of the derogatory tone this was taking, and he took a few hesitant steps forward. Forcibly he summoned all his self-assertion, self-esteem, and self-control, and managed to say, "What?" in a sort of pale, questioning meow. The cat raised its eyebrows at him.

"What, indeed," said the cat. "'What' says he."

"Commonly," said one of the sisters, stroking the cat back to silence, "people are rather inclined to jeer at us for a bit before they understand our position."

"Kept underground," said the other. "Kept like cats." The cat rumbled. "Kept like mice, then," she corrected herself."

"Perhaps I'm not the jeering type," said Axford, somewhat hollowly.

"N-n-no—" said Noughts thoughtfully. "I don't think that's it."

"I think you understand us," said Crosses quietly.

Axford stood very still, because he did. He understood exactly what they were, and knew that he stood before the most powerful beings in all Wonderland. He wasn't quite sure what had tipped him off, but something had. Perhaps it was something to do with the silence in the room, that song they seemed to sing without moving their mouths, or their wise eyes, or the fact that the Queen kept them in the basement. After a moment, he blurted out a question that had been on his mind for some time— since, in fact, before they had even met the Queen.

"Why were the walls laughing at me?" he demanded, then, as an afterthought, "Please, sorry, thank you?"

The sisters regarded him with amusement.

"Because they know all about you," they said. "They know your destiny."

"But *I* don't know my destiny."

"Oh dear," said Crosses. "I'm afraid that rather gives a clue as to your intellect as compared to that of stationary, wall-like objects."

"Don't worry about it, though," said Noughts warmly. "It's really up to you in any case. And you weren't born clairvoyant, we can see that, whereas the walls were built like that."

The confusion Axford felt was plain to be seen on his face, and Crosses, who saw the words *Who is Claire Voyant?* rising to his lips, coughed discreetly and said, before he could get the fatal phrase out, "You can't see the unseen, hear the unheard, foreknow the future, that sort of thing."

"Oh," said Axford, greatly relieved in his mind. "Of course not."

"Which leaves it up to us to tell you," said Noughts.

And they did.

Axford thought it over.

"So, we're not doomed?"

Crosses laughed. "Far from it."

"And when Alice gets here— our savior and all that— will everything go back to the way it was?"

"Nothing ever goes back to the way it was," said Noughts. "And whether it becomes better or worse depends upon—"

'Me?' said Axford resignedly.

Noughts delicately placed the tips of her fingers together. "Not exactly."

"Oh," he said, and deflated.

"It depends in a large part upon the Alice herself."

"*The* Alice?"

"And upon the Queen, and upon your friend the raven, and upon Fred, and upon the rabbit—"

"Hold on, hold on, hold on," said Axford, throwing his hands up in the air, clearly suffering from information overload. "Who is Fred and who is the rabbit?"

A single slight frown crossed both identical faces, sliding from right to left without stopping.

"Sometimes the things unseen aren't entirely clear," Crosses said. "Apparently, someone named Fred is going to show up, someone unlike anyone ever seen in Wonderland before. And he's going to be important."

"Yes," agreed Noughts, "Fred is going to be very big when he gets here."

"And as for the rabbit— well, you'll find that out before too long. The Queen will show you."

Axford raised an eyebrow. "Oh, he's to do with the Queen, eh?"

"Well, he works for us, really—"

"But only the Queen can let him out of his cage."

He shook his head and sighed. "Do we have to feed him carrots?"

"*Dear* Axford," said the sisters through their peals of laughter. Even the giant cat snickered at him. "He's not *that* kind of rabbit."

Death was getting irritated. This rarely happened. It hadn't, in fact, happened in hundreds of years.

And it was all because of that *girl*.

If Death had possessed a face, it would have looked moody and sullen and love-struck. As it was, he had to make do with kicking a rock back and forth, in a moody and sullen and love-struck manner. It's difficult for something without physical feet to connect with a rock, so he had to do it with his mind, and it wasn't exactly the same. He kept getting distracted, and his timing was off— the rock would scuttle away a few minutes after the space that would have been his foot, had he had one, touched it. Or not touched it, exactly. Not touched at all, in fact.

The rock was getting nervous.

"What is it?" Death said aloud. "What can I do? Flowers? Candy? Getting down on one knee and singing *'Love Me Tender'*?"

Of course, in order to do that, he'd have to have a knee. Never mind learning all the words, he never could remember that middle part, hmm-hmm something something.

This led him to an entirely different issue entirely.

"Would she find me more attractive," he asked, for lack of better companionship, the rock, "if I had a body?"

This required some serious thinking on his part, and he set to with a will. After a while, he decided to go visit a friend of his; or rather, perhaps not a "friend" exactly, but certainly a prior acquaintance.

Presumably, if it was the body she needed, she'd prefer a good-looking one. Death's idea of good looks, when it came down to it, was a bit odd. This is only to be expected in someone who has seen centuries of humans come and go, along with their ever-changing peculiar ideas of what constitutes beauty. He'd been perpetually amazed at how much importance was placed on appearance, when clearly it was the mind that mattered. Well, to be perfectly frank, he was also amazed that so much importance was placed on *anything*, when clearly everything was transitory anyway. But, all told, he had rather more appreciation for a keen mind than a face or form.

The friend who was really just an acquaintance he went to see was a nearly-forty Sussex farmer/undertaker/playboy who answered to the name F. F. Killjoy and, in fact, practically anything you wanted to call him, provided you were female and under thirty. He didn't get called all that often, as a matter of fact, which was why he still went to bed single every night. He had wide blue eyes and a long narrow nose and when he wasn't talking he wasn't bad-looking— but he was always talking.

Even now.

"Get away from me," he cried, brandishing— at least, he liked to think of what he was doing as brandishing, though really a proper brandisher doesn't shake like a paint mixing machine in an earthquake— a pitchfork.

"Come on," Death pleaded. "I'll give it right back."

"Not on your life," yelled Mr. F. F. Killjoy, not quite realizing what an oxymoron that was, though thinking at the time that it sounded decidedly odd. He'd had a lot to do with death, being an undertaker, but wasn't all that good coping just at the moment, for which he can probably be forgiven.

"I don't really have to have your permission, you know," said Death, and added, "it's only out of politeness I ask at all."

"I won't give it up," vowed F.F. Killjoy. He tightened his grip on the pitchfork, hands slippery with sweat. This had not been a good day. This was, in fact, continuing not to be a good day.

"Now, come on, man—"

"But I've got a date Thursday!"

"Oh," said Death, relieved, "is that all? Right, well, I promise to have it back to you by Thursday. Now, kindly shut up."

Death snapped his fingers.

The mind of F. F. Killjoy went Somewhere Else. It was a worrying place and it was not at all happy there. But that doesn't really matter.

In this one exceptional case, it was not the mind that mattered, but the body.

It was tall, much taller than Axford, tall as any full-grown human. It wore the ceremonial waistcoat, with a golden watch chain rather ostentatiously displayed, and looked uncomfortable in it. It twitched its nose.

"Oh," said Axford. "*That* kind of rabbit."

Everyone else had undergone their session with the twins. None of them said what they'd talked about, but then, none of them came out as cheerfully as Axford had. They came out, for the most part, sniffing and wiping their eyes and shaking all over. All but Eldritch Rune, the lone Fiendish, who came out looking thoughtful.

Once everyone had gone through the ordeal, the Queen had pulled a rabbit out of her hat.

"Party trick," thought Axford disapprovingly.

It was a large rabbit, but then, it had been a huge hat. The Queen subscribed avidly to the Hat of the Month club there in town. She'd been a member for years, and every month the hats had gotten bigger. The particular one she'd used had been, in a former life, a bathtub for a sixteen-ton gorilla, and when she wore it a platoon of servants had to hold it up around the edges so it wouldn't squish her like a bug. Even so, it had split almost imperceptibly along the seams as the rabbit struggled out.

He stood and blinked through his spectacles-on-a-stick at them.

"May I present," said the Queen, looking bored, "Geoffrey, a direct descendant of the very first White Rabbit, who of course is alive and well in his cage at the Museum, and who sends his best wishes, presumably. He is *not* for eating," she continued in an abrupt shout, shooting a daggered glare at one of the chimeras.

The chimera shrugged, and looked sulky. "How do you know until you've tried it?"

"Best wait till we can get a good fire going and put it in a stew," advised its friend.

"With potatoes and celery," said the Carpenter hopefully.

The chimeras eyed him and moved off.

"How are we supposed to scare everyone when *he's* around?" one muttered.

"Yeah, it's not fair to put a professional in the game."

"I'm now conducing sea-side tours weekly," the Carpenter announced. "I'll give you one for free if you know the secret handshake."

Everyone shuffled away from him till he was in the center of a circle all by himself.

"Er, hullo," said Geoffrey.

His voice was rather thick and nasal, which was only to be expected considering the flatness of his nose, and he was exceedingly polite. He didn't seem to know precisely why he was there. He made an awkward, self-conscious little bow.

"Hullo," he said again, "er, peoples."

Axford was automatically allergic to anyone who said "peoples," and he sneezed violently at this point. Everyone else said, "Hullo, Geoffrey."

Geoffrey said, "Hullo," again.

"Aha," thought Axford, "a real wit." Aloud he said, "What exactly are you for?"

"It's, er, rather an honorary position," said the rabbit. "But the Queen seems to feel I should be joining you on your, er, quest. Er, impossible mission."

"Solemn duty by you undertaken," said the Queen. A very distinct look of irritation was creeping into her eyes. The raven swooned with this demonstration of unsuspected knowledge of its own language. The Queen had just been trying to sound impressive.

"And so well anyway then," said the rabbit, very quickly, "I'll just be going along with you— I suppose." He did not look entirely happy about this, but scuffed the ground with one long foot.

"And here," announced her Majesty, "is my—"

She clapped a hand over her own mouth for a moment, eyes wide. Then she removed it, and swallowed, taking another moment to compose herself.

"Dog," she finished.

"Why do I get the feeling that's not what she started out to say?" inquired Cheesebread in a low voice.

"Shh," snapped the raven, who would brook no criticism of its beloved.

But *there* was the dog. And not the large hell-hounds that trailed after the Queen as protection when she left the castle, either. She'd left those in the kennel on account of an unfortunate incident a few days ago when they'd come very close to eating Geoffrey.

No, this dog was different. It was very small, and it trotted from behind the throne and stood to one side of the Queen's ankles and looked at them all with crossed eyes.

"Its name is Comfit," said the Queen. "It's a Shi'Tzu."

"Not a very nice thing to call it," muttered Axford, "a Shi'Tzu."

"Comfit will be accompanying you as my delegate, a representative of the royal house."

"Yup," said Comfit, straining to uncross its eyes.

"A talking Shi'Tzu," said Eldritch Rune. "How interesting."

He did not sound interested in the least.

"Interestingly, I'm sure it'll be a great help to you," said the Queen. She did not sound interested, either. Nor did she sound as though she actually believed that this small talking dog would be of help to the Looking-For-Alice delegation.

"Kibble?" said Comfit hopefully, looking up adoringly at the Queen. The Queen sneered down at it.

"I believe I'll appoint a royal dog-watcher," she said decidedly. She looked over the line of prisoners and her eyes glowed.

"Freaky," said the raven, and shivered.

"You," the Queen commanded, and pointed a red fingernail at Axford, who tried to hide behind Rune. He would have been successful, except the dog followed him and made a sudden violent leap. Suddenly, Axford had an armful of Shi'Tzu.

He was glad it was a little dog. He got a better grip on Comfit and tried to make it stop licking his face.

The Queen observed him with a cool, triumphant smile. Axford stood up straight and tried to look capable and superior. Superior to the dog, anyway, if nothing else. He was worried about it, as it didn't seem to be working out quite as he planned.

Of course, very little ever did.

The dog found his eyebrows and settled to a slow, steady licking motion that started at his left temple and ran across both brows. Axford suppressed a grimace, figured that this didn't help much, really, and growled at the dog, who put its tongue back in its mouth and looked surprised at him.

"You half dog or something?" it said.

"No."

"You bite?"

"*Yes.*"

The dog shrugged.

"I don't. I find that, in the long run, niceness beats cruelty."

"That so," said Axford, gritting his teeth.

"That's so. Cruelty always comes back to bite you in the tail." Comfit tossed a careful glance over its shoulder at its mistress, who was pretending not to watch. It heaved a sigh and turned back to Axford with a businesslike air. "You have kibble?"

"No, I do not."

"There's your problem, then."

"Time you all started out," said the Queen, with a delicately royal smirk. "Follow me."

They followed her because, as usual, it wasn't a request, but a command.

Chapter Five

It wasn't a bad body, as physical bodies went. Six foot tall, or as near as mattered anyhow. 168 pounds. Big blue eyes, one slightly lazy: only they were fairly well grey now. Auburn hair: had been going grey at the temples, now going fairly well grey all over. An articulate nose and clever eyebrows. A smooth-skinned, glassy face, with a large mole high up on one cheekbone which Death automatically noted as a cancer hazard. The skin, already pale, had gone rather colorless now. Rather grey, really. When Death had taken over, the color of the whole body had faded dramatically, running down the skin and dripping to the floor in a slightly steaming, multicolored puddle of liquid that dissolved within seconds and appeared later that day as a small rainbow over Sussex.

The robes were too big. When he'd arrived back at his home, he'd taken off the undertaker's blue jeans, plaid shirt, and socks, and put the customary robes on. Then he'd started to wish he'd found a body that was closer to seven feet, though this would have required a more thorough search. The main section of the robe was absurdly baggy, the sleeves reached far down over his long-fingered hands, the hems dragged in folds on the ground. He flipped the cowl up over his head, and it fell straight down, covering his face, so he was wrapped in darkness. He was abruptly, absurdly claustrophobic.

This, he reckoned, probably stemmed from some ridiculous psychological reaction induced in this body he'd borrowed. He didn't understand the human fear of the dark, he'd spent most of his time without any light at all and enjoyed every minute—

He neglected to take the cowl off in time, not used to responding to hints from his human structure, and he felt sweat starting on his forehead. He ripped the hood off in a sudden blind panic.

Thud-thud, said his human heart. Rather too quickly, he thought, though of course he was used to a very, very slow heartbeat. Nearly imperceptible, in fact.

He forgot to breathe for a minute or two and experienced the wonderful effects of that.

After he was done coughing and breathing in as deep as possible, he thought, *Humans. How do they live?*

Of course, when he was around, they tended not to.

He adjusted the robes so they weren't trapping his feet, and took a few steps forward. It worked.

He felt an interesting sensation engulf the muscles of his face. The human body whispered to him that it was a smile. He'd never really seen a smile, and certainly never felt one, because they were not available in plenty when he was in the vicinity.

There was a mirror upon the wall opposite him, an odd thing to be seen in the house of a being with no physical body. It was evidence, he hoped, of his own uniquely quirky sense of humor. He was perfectly accustomed to seeing only a robe floating above the ground, with no attendant flesh or bone. Well, well. How times changed.

He looked into it. It was rather a fiendish smile he'd acquired, the teeth sharp as a vampire's and oddly attractive in a way that seemed to be trying to sell something. He was quite pleased with it.

He took a few more steps. It still worked. He experienced triumph. Perhaps being human wasn't all bad.

He took another step. He experienced euphoric giggling.

He took another step.

He took another step, tripped over his robes, and landed on his newly-acquired face.

He experienced pain.

The things he did for Breca, he thought. The things she had better do for him.

"Explain this to us," said Axford. "We don't get it."

"How difficult can it be?" said the Queen, exasperated.

"Very, actually." Axford found that most things could be quite difficult if one tried hard enough.

"You all know the legend."

They all knew the legend, and indicated as much, with much enthusiastic nodding. There wasn't an ant's daughter in Wonderland who hadn't heard the legend from each of her mother's six knees.

"Well, there's a mercy anyhow," she said. "Now, this is where she came down. Obviously, in order to find her, you have to go up."

Axford looked at the rope in front of him. It stretched up and up into the darkness far above them, where it disappeared, though presumably it still went up above that.

"Couldn't it have been a rope *ladder*?" he said.

"Weakling!" spat the Queen. "Did you never have Archaic Physical Education in schools?"

"I failed," said Axford simply. He meant the whole of school, not just Arc. Phys. Ed., but did not feel like elaborating at the moment.

The Queen rolled her eyes. "Quit complaining and get climbing, or I'll see you back to your cell, and you won't be getting out this time.'

Rope, cell, thought Axford to himself, weighing his few possibilities against each other. *Rope, cell. Rope— cell.*

He took a look at the line of prisoners behind him. His eyes settled on Eldritch Rune, who, as in all his unguarded moments, looked lonely.

He turned back, wrapped both hands around the rope, and began to climb.

Geoffrey the rabbit stood behind them all, alongside the Queen.

"Er," he said. "Er."

"What is it?" she snapped, turning on him as though he was an obnoxious mail-carrier asking for a raise.

"Er, how do I get up?"

"Climb," she said. She decided to speak using only as of the few muscles in her face as possible. If this made her difficult to understand, so much the better.

Geoffrey cast a glance down at his paws, large and furry and not the least bit useful for gripping a rope. A wordless glance, but it was perfectly understandable.

"What do you expect me to do?" the Queen said irritably. "Give you a piggy-back ride?"

She stalked off.

"Queeney-back ride," Geoffrey editorialized behind her with a soft and distressed voice. Comfit the talking Shi'Tzu glanced up at him, then turned and followed her.

"How do I get up?" it yipped.

"Basket," she said shortly.

"Ah."

"And you'd better keep an eye on them. Especially that beardless dwarf. He makes me uneasy."

Comfit quite liked Axford, actually. Certainly he kept his eyebrows very clean. But he reasoned that everyone was entitled to their own opinion, and let it be.

Geoffrey got up eventually, using a complicated system involving a spring board, a creature on the other end hauling on the main rope, lots of other ropes, and several fervent prayers. Geoffrey looked very embarrassed by all this, but there wasn't a great deal he could do.

Comfit went up last, fielding a wink from the Queen, who thought back to the tense moment when she had introduced the dog and nearly said, "*This is my spy.*" That tended to be the way it went, she found: she would be making a statement and thinking to herself, "Do NOT say this. Do NOT say this," and then when she got up in front of people, "This," would be the first thing that came out of her mouth, whatever "This" was in that instance. Occasionally, of course, it was "That." Did that happen to many people? Surely not. It was a ridiculously inefficient way to speak. The Queen shivered. She'd very nearly been a fool.

She watched as the basket ascended to the heights above, being slowly swallowed up in darkness.

And then, because she was left alone, she laughed.

She laughed all the way back down the rose garden paths, stepping on a few of the flowers, who shrieked in pain and tried to bite her calves, but they were too slow and she was long gone. She laughed as she entered the castle proper. Her laughter echoed eerily in the lower passageways of the castle keep. She was still laughing when she reached the lonely room wherein sat Noughts and Crosses, two sisters with Intuition, who saw and heard everything, knew everything, except for the certain identity of one Fred. And even that they had their suspicions about.

"They're off," said the Queen. "They're off. Thank you, dear sisters—"

She swept them an exaggerated bow. A thought struck her in the middle of it, and she stood up straight.

"Incidentally," she said, "you told me one of them would prove themselves to be something beyond all expectation. Which one was it?"

"I suppose you'll just have to wait till they come back," said Noughts, watching her with cool eyes, "and anyway you wouldn't believe us if we told you."

"Ah, so they will come back then."

"Some of them."

The Queen moistened her lips. "Successfully?"

"Not entirely," said Noughts after a moment. Crosses closed her eyes suddenly as though her head hurt, and clutched the cat on her lap closer. The cat made a sound halfway between a murmur and a meow.

"Tell me this then, O sisters two," said the Queen, who was quite used to getting non-answers but didn't like them any more for that. "Will the Kingdom become happy?"

Noughts scrutinized her closely for a moment. Then—

"Yes," she said.

The Queen relaxed, though she hadn't realized till that moment that she'd been holding herself stiff in anticipation. She tried a smile, and despite aesthetic evidence to the contrary was quite pleased with it.

"Well," she said, "that solves both our problems, then, doesn't it?"

Crosses opened her eyes very suddenly and fixed them on the Queen. They went straight through her skinny body and reached whatever lump of rock passed for a heart, so the Queen was suddenly deeply disturbed.

"She said the Kingdom will be happy, you know," said Crosses. "She didn't say anything about you."

The Queen's face did a slow sort of crashing trick that was quite impressive. She took a moment to compose herself, straightening up and putting her hands on her hips. "Well, will I be unhappy?" she pressed.

Noughts looked like she didn't want to admit it, but finally the words forced themselves out. No, the Queen would not be unhappy—

Her Majesty smiled her familiar triumphant smile at Crosses. All that worry and stress for nothing.

"There," she said, "you see?"

—and in fact not much was said about the Queen one way or another—

"I told you, didn't I?"

— almost as if at some point in the proceedings the Queen would cease to exist. Which was puzzling, because such a thing simply did not happen in Wonderland.

But the Queen wasn't listening. She swept them another mocking bow, so low she had to clap a hasty hand to her crown to prevent it falling off, and then she left.

Noughts turned to Crosses and said, "It's got to be something to do with this Fred person. Someone or something who can set a mind in a sort of state of— *unbeing*." She squinted at her sister. "Are you sure you can't see anything?"

"No, I can't," said Crosses, petting her cat, shaking her head. "No, but I can guess."

"Me-*ouch*," said the cat, serenely.

Chapter Six

Axford Barrel sat on a rock in a different world from the one he'd lived in all his life, and the first thing he noticed was that his feet touched the ground.

This struck him as odd. Not odd that this was the first thing he noticed, but odd that this first thing he noticed was there to be noticed at all.

It was a big rock. If things had been as usual, his feet would have been swinging in midair.

Things, then, were not as usual.

Hmm.

There was a surprise.

Perhaps, he thought, this world was fundamentally smaller than Wonderland, and so he seemed bigger in it.

But as he watched the rest of the prisoners— no, not prisoners any longer, but bold brave questors, or integrity-seeking loyal lawmen of the Queen, or simply ex-prisoners if one wished to be truthful— emerge from the hole in the ground, he began to doubt, for the non-human features of each were slowly melting away. Even the chimeras took on human form, and their fur thinned drastically and became hair. The Fiendish Thingies all lost their snouts— they sank into their faces till they had perfectly normal, if rather large, human noses.

Even the spider developed two long, thin arms, two long, thin legs, and a shifty expression. Even, good lord, even the rabbit became human. Ish. The vest and pocket watch were thankfully augmented by more traditional clothing.

All but the raven, who seemed as usual, and the dog, who leapt from the basket, scampered over to Axford, and jumped into his arms.

The dog seemed much smaller.

No, it was that Axford was much bigger.

Or was he?

How do I *know?* he asked himself, irritated. He looked up from his internal monologue and found that nearly everyone else was revolting. (No, not *that* kind of revolting.) They were joyfully finding uses for brand-new opposable thumbs and tying the rabbit up. The rabbit was not happy about it.

The rabbit, thought Axford, made a very ugly man. But then, he hadn't been a particularly handsome rabbit. Oh well.

"What are you doing?"

"Tying the rabbit," said one of the former-chimeras. His face had an exceedingly blank expression that was more due to nature than cultivation and which would have been useful to him in a career as a poker player, or a lawyer.

"Yes," said Axford, "this I can see. Why?"

"Well," said the chimera, thoughtfully, "we got to thinking, you see, and—"

"Thinking," said Axford, taking a deep breath and letting it out slowly, shaking his head. "Not good, in this case."

In Wonderland, the chimera would have eaten Axford's head without another thought. As it was, they were both human now, and both men, and, the chimera noted with sudden worry, they were both the same size, about five foot eight or so.

"And we got to thinking," the chimera continued, contenting himself with a frosty glare, "that there's not much point to this looking-for-Alice thing. Who's to guarantee, if we go back, that the Queen won't put us straight back in the cells? I say, we're free, we run for it."

There was a murmur of agreement.

"Aha," thought Axford, "crowd action." He'd had experience with mobs, as well as pitchforks and lighted lantern, as a result of a costume experiment when he was younger. He knew how these things tended to go. "Look," he said aloud, "just because you *think* she'll put you back in, doesn't mean she *will*."

There was a small silence afterwards, in which Axford realized he had just made what was possibly the weakest point in the history of arguments.

"Right, that's it then," he said resignedly. "First sign of trouble, you abandon your homeland and head for the hills. All you're concerned with is your so-called better life. You don't care a slug on a banana leaf for the life you had before." This was saying something, as some of the convicts had eaten a slug on a banana leaf after breakfast that very morning. They were handed out like mints in the Queen's dungeons. "*Think* about it. *Think* about how beautiful Wonderland was when Alice was there, how lovely, how incredible, how amazing, how— how *wonderful*! And you're willing to jeopardize all that because you *think* you might land in a jail cell?"

There seemed to be only one response to this, and the chimera gave it.

"Yes," it said. "Goodbye."

They turned to go.

"But what about my destiny?" howled Axford suddenly, taking himself by surprise. He found that he was breathing very fast and very hard. He was, it seemed, far more involved in this whole thing than he had originally thought. He felt, in fact, more serious about this than he'd ever been about almost anything, and this was a deep and unsettling realization.

"It's not *my* destiny," said the chimera, with the lofty ambivalence of the truly unconcerned, and lead the way. They went off, leaving Axford and all claim to residency in Wonderland, behind. In the years to come they all mixed in fairly easily with human society, which probably explains some of those relatives you've never been exactly sure about.

Dap-Hodil and Cheesebread paused and cast him doubtful looks.

"Won't you stay?" Axford pleaded. "We've *got* to do this."

"We are staying," said Cheesebread. "We're staying here on Alice's world. Wonderland's great, sure, but I can't take the people. Look at me *here*, though," he said, gesturing. He was about five foot seven, now, his ears were considerably less pointed, and though he still wore gnomish clothing, that's something he could change easily, and very shortly would. "Look at Dap-Hodil." Dap-Hodil had himself shrunk to six and a half feet, smaller bones, less lean and wolfish. "We've got a chance here, see. We can be *normal* here. Everyone goes on about how wonderful Wonderland was when Alice was there. Nobody thinks about what Alice's world must be like— a whole *world* full of Alices. What could be better?"

Despite himself, Axford could very easily see what Cheesebread was trying to say. The very thought of it caught at his imagination with soft hands and a stubborn grip. He shook his head to come back to himself, away from a world full of Alices, and to reach out to his destiny again, home in Wonderland.

"Alright," he said desperately. "Alright, that's fine, stay here if you want, only help me find Alice first."

Cheesebread and Dap-Hodil exchanged glances. It was much easier now there was less of a height difference.

"Well," said Cheesebread, doubtfully, "I suppose we could do that—"

Suddenly, with the addition of a few extra pairs of eyes, Axford's destiny seemed within reach again. He grinned vastly, swung round to look at the raven, and found Eldritch Rune waiting there alongside the bird.

"You're staying too?" he asked.

The Fiendish shrugged a little, almost as though embarrassed. "After all,' he said. "According to the twins, it's my destiny too."

"Great!" said Axford, not missing a beat. "Untie the rabbit."

Geoffrey the rabbit-man was duly freed. He stood stiffly, trembling slightly from the deep physical and mental distress of being in such a situation, plucking at the "Kick Me" sign some wag had stuck to his back, and managed a weak smile and a faltering thank you.

"Okay," said Axford. "Let's go."

"Aha," said Geoffrey, with a fearful glance at his surroundings. He held up a finger and glanced at it in surprise. "Well, if it's all the same to you, I won't, thank you. I believe I'll just— believe I'll just— stay here and, er, guard the hole."

He stepped as close to the rabbit hole as he could without falling into it, and flashed a sheepish smile at Axford, pulling the traditional pocket-watch out of his pocket and checking it to be sure of the time of their departure.

"Suit yourself," said Axford, now all fired up and ready to go, and fully realizing that a frightened rabbit-man would not be much help in this sort of quest. "Coming?" he said to the world at large, in too much of a hurry to address each of his companions separately. Without waiting, he plunged haphazardly down the path, tripping several times over roots and plants that were in his way because he couldn't be bothered to watch where he was going. He was pursuing fate, a sport followed by the majority of humanity, though most of them remain oblivious to the fact that this is what they are, in fact, doing.

"Boy, what's with him?" asked Cheesebread. He was mostly talking to Eldritch Rune, since Rune seemed to know what was going on, but it was Dap-Hodil who said, "How should I know?" and when Cheesebread turned he saw Rune starting to his feet and hurrying at a great pace after Axford.

"Would you look at that," he said, though really he wasn't at all surprised. "What's gotten into those two?"

"Erm," said the raven, who had a pretty good idea. "Destiny calls."

They met up with each other at a crossroads, and agreed to split up and look for Alice, and meet later at the local pub. "Remember," cautioned Axford, "it's been nine years, so likely she looks a little different, but she's got to be around here someplace, right?"

So Axford and the raven went to the left, with Comfit the dog tagging along behind. Cheesebread and Dap-Hodil went to the right, and Rune, alone, squared his shoulders, sniffed, and went straight ahead.

Of all their adventures that day, only one in particular was of any importance, and this is it.

Remy Starkey was twenty-five, had red hair and wide blue eyes and a patient expression.

This is a partial record of what she thought as she woke up that morning.

"Oh, far too much light, forgot to draw *big* the curtains hmm must have been *nose* distracted what an odd dream (snatches of a song) have to *big* get up quick, I'm *nose* late and work because *big* its not like *nose* I've got a fortune to sit and *big* rest on *nose* do I or do I not *big* want breakfast *nose* is it worth it, all this eating stuff?"

At this point she looked in her bathroom mirror and thought *Big nose. Mine.*

It wasn't, in point of fact, that big. Remy was of Welsh descent and she, for no particular reason, put it down to that, though a friend of hers had once told her that it was because of sins she had committed in a previous life. Remy was a very laid-back individual but this 'friend' had soon ceased to be one.

In reality, which she was only distantly acquainted with, Remy's nose was no more than slightly out of the ordinary— this was actually a good thing, as the majority of people in her little corner of England had noses that were slightly inadequate as far as actually breathing went, which was probably why their mouths were open so much of the time. A much more friend-like friend of hers had explained this to her as Remy's nose not actually being so big— it was only that everyone else's nose was so small. Size, she'd been told many times over, was relative; aunts and uncles, specifically.

The nose belonging to the man who walked into Remy's workplace that morning was a welcome wonder indeed.

She looked up. "Wow," she said, where she'd meant to say, "Hi." And then, because this was a barbershop and she was the barber on duty at the moment, she went on.

"Would you like me to cut your nose— er, hair— er," she said, because she was distracted. He was a very good-looking man, she thought, very clean-cut, not like the usual goatee-wearing, multi-pierced scumbags she got in here. Though, of course, that really only made it all the worse.

The man, bless him, took no notice of her confusion and acute embarrassment. He merely looked at her with soulful brown eyes and said, in a beautiful voice, "I was looking for Alice."

"Alice?" Aha! A name. Not *his* name, but a name. "I, er, don't *think* she's here—"

Her voice was doubtful, out of sheer politeness, and they both pretended to look around the empty shop for a moment.

"Ah, well, I suppose she'll be somewhere else," said the man vaguely, and began to turn round.

"Wait," said Remy desperately. "Wait— ah—" she added as he turned back and looked expectantly at her. This demanded a follow-up. "I'll go and ask the boys in the back, they may— have some knowledge— of the whereabouts— of, er, Alice. Er— or perhaps you'd like to ask them yourself?"

He quirked a questioning eyebrow at her, which she took for a yes and turned and yelled to the back room, "Lenin, would you mind coming out a minute?"

Lenin came, shuffling and slow. He was about sixty years old, had thoughtful eyes, and seemed to have difficulty calling his mind back from his alternate existence as a pioneer of economical reform. He was followed by two other men, one tall and thin, one shorter and slightly lachrymose.

"You called," said Lenin with a lugubrious peacefulness.

"Yes, well, Lenin, and boys, this gentleman—"

She suddenly lit on a way to find out the man's name— asking for it for the purpose of making introductions. Very clever. Very tricky. Why didn't she think of it before?

"Ah, sir," she said with a smile, turning back to the man with the wondrous nose, "I didn't catch your name."

"I didn't throw it," said the man with the wondrous nose, blinking in puzzlement. "But it's Eldritch Rune, in any case."

"How nice," she smiled, "and, er, this is my boss, Mr. Lenin, and my associate Max Artney, and the shop-boy, Arthur Harrison—"

"Hullo," said Eldritch Rune, bobbing his head at them. "Er, I was looking for Alice."

The men regarded him seriously for a moment.

"Never heard of him," said Lenin dourly, and went back in the rear room.

"Sorry," said the other two, with expansive shrugs.

"Likewise," said Rune, and nodded his thanks at them. He turned to go. Remy bit her lip. He was walking out, of the shop and out of her life—

"Oh, Max," she said, somewhat desperately, "couldn't we give him a free cut? Just, you know, because?"

"Free isn't really free, ever," Max reminded her.

"But can't we, just this once?"

Max Artney looked from her to Arthur, who shrugged.

"On your head be it then," he told Remy, who grinned and raced after Rune. She dragged him back in, promising all sorts of wonders she felt sure she could deliver. Once she'd seated him, she set to with a will.

She felt quite at ease with him, which was a nice change from how things usually were, but despite all that, she hadn't forgotten how to be self-conscious. She didn't seem to be able to forget.

Rune watched her in silence and wondered why this slightly peculiar woman kept trying to hide her face behind towels and scissors.

She cut his hair swiftly and neatly and tried not to think about his profile because it made her ridiculously nervous, and gave her a continuous thrill from the soles of her feet upwards. When she was done she swung him to face the mirror and jumped a little at his sudden start.

"Don't you like it?"

"Is that *me*?" he gasped, staring at his reflection.

"Well, it's a mirror, see," she said. "So it must be. What's wrong?"

"Nothing," said Eldritch Rune, dazedly. He hadn't quite realized the change in himself when he came to Alice's world, the change due to the Queen's behest, so that they might have a better time of the searching. "Nothing, nothing, it's just— you made me look so— so *human*."

"Ah," she said, and gave a short and silly little laugh which she immediately regretted. "Well, that's only natural, really."

He stood up, turned to look at her and smiled. "Thank you very much."

"Oh, my pleasure." His smile was reflected right back at him.

"You never told me your name."

"Starkey," she said, fiddling with her nails. "Remy Starkey."

"Starkey Remy Starkey," he repeated with another warm smile, then suddenly stopped cold and gave her a long look during which she felt her insteps melting and began randomly wondering about feet of clay.

"Come away with me," he said, with a sudden amount of urgency.

Remy needed no second bidding.

If it had taken him any longer, she wouldn't have needed a first.

Chapter Seven

Axford sat on a stool and looked dejected. He'd been searching all day, to no avail.

"Alice," he'd said to the people. "You know Alice? Where is she?"

The people had looked at him as though he'd suddenly sprouted wings. This was not unusual in Wonderland, though presumably spontaneous wing-growing was considered odd, here on Alice's world. This reaction seemed to be nearly universal, apart from one old man, who'd cocked his head at him for a moment and looked first wise, then, gradually, more and more confused, until he finally shook his head and walked away, his head still turned at an unnatural angle.

So Axford had given up for a while. He made his way to the pub where they'd agreed to meet. It was extremely hot inside, and noisy, with tinges of violence, but Axford welcomed it. It fit the mood he was in.

The raven perched on his shoulder and pecked annoyingly at his hair; the dog scrabbled up onto Axford's lap and immediately slid off. The barkeeper looked at him and raised his eyebrow.

"You work at the zoo?"

"Yessir," said Axford, bobbing his head. "Left my llama at home though, sir. She doesn't like the damp."

"Jolly good," said the barkeeper after a pause, but it sounded idiotic, because he was American.

Axford found that he was sitting next to a girl who was gloomily demanding salted peanuts, which he didn't like (the proximity, not the peanuts) but had no choice about. The pub was crowded and lively with people in pre-drink distress, orders being mixed up and faultily delivered with an incompetence bordering on the supernatural.

Cheesebread and Dap-Hodil arrived. Cheesebread sat next to Axford, and Dap-Hodil, after a perfunctory nod, went back outside to look for a chicken to chase. He'd been desperately bored all day.

"Find her?" said Cheesebread, gloomily depositing his elbow on the counter and his chin on his hand.

"No. You?"

"No."

That was about what they'd been expecting. As wondrous and different as Alice's world had proved to be, it was also a bit manky in places. They'd found most of these places, in fact, during the course of the day and had long since ceased to be excited or optimistic about things. They sat and nodded to themselves, cynical and unsurprised.

Cheesebread looked for something to occupy himself. On his left was Axford, and on his right was a tall woman of generally extensive proportions. She also came equipped with serious brown hair and somber brown eyes. She resisted his attempts to buy her a drink, but only on general principles, it seemed, for she accepted the money he put down on the counter to pay for it.

"Pubkeeper," said Axford loudly. He was nervous and unhappy suddenly and he knew his voice would shake if he didn't say things in the manner of a peevish king. "Pubkeeper!"

"Bartender," stage-whispered Cheesebread.

"Oh yes, thank you. Bartender!"

The bartender looked and didn't like what he saw. Two of them now, he thought. Not likely to have any money, either, from the look of their clothes.

Axford recognized that look. He'd seen it on Soul Train's face many times. He pulled someone else's money from the depths of his pocket and flipped through it carelessly. He looked up to see the bartender grinning at him as though all his cares and woes had suddenly vanished, ice melted in the sun.

"An ale for my friend and me."

"One or two?" The bartender was confused.

"Two," said Axford, blinking, because in his own mind it had been perfectly clear.

The bartender went off and pulled four pints.

"That'll do," said Axford, who couldn't be bothered to bother. Struck by a sudden thought, he looked at the man with keen eyes and said, "Tell me, sir. Do you know a lot of people around here?"

"Oh yeah, yeah. Everyone. Small town, you know, and I've been here— oh, nearly six years now."

"Indeed," said Axford, delighted. "Tell me, then. Do you know of a young woman by the name of Alice?"

"Alice?" said the bartender. There came the acrid smell of mental gears barking against each other's shins in their efforts to get under way. Axford blanched. Maybe it was the man's breath.

"Alice," he repeated (nothing ventured, nothing daunted, he thought, though perhaps it was the other way round). "Small, I think. Blondish, brownish, hairish hair. Blue eyes. Small nose, curly hair, I believe, on her head, that is, and did I mention rather small? She was only somewhere in the vicinity of six to eight years old."

"Mmmph," said the bartender, like a bull confronted by a talking mayfly.

"Of course I've never met her myself. Like I said, she was about six, nine years ago, I think." Axford gave a sudden sharp embarrassed grin. "I'm not entirely sure."

"Mmmmph," said the bartender, like a bullfrog assaulted by a tap-dancing gnat.

"Rather famous, I believe, around these parts—" Axford went on, hopelessly.

Suddenly the bartender's countenance brightened and he gave him a knowing look. "Ahh," he said. "*Alice.*"

"Yes?" said Axford. He leaned forward on the top of the bar.

"As in Alice in *Wonderland.*"

"Yes, you know it?" said Axford, with a quick and delighted grin.

"Get people asking for her all the time in this town."

"Oh?"

"Asking all kinds of stuff about her, sure. I guess you think it's funny." The bartender gave an undignified snort, to show exactly how funny *he* thought it was.

Axford shut his mouth tightly and stared intently at him. The bartender's broad sneer began to slowly crash down and transform into something totally other.

"You're serious?" he finally managed.

Nothing, said Axford, only nodded silently.

"Well— I dunno, sir— it's been so long, see— way before my time."

Axford blinked. The bartender, he estimated shrewdly, must be at least in his forties. And it had been only nine years since Alice left, in Wonderland.

"Old Alice must be long dead, sir. I'm sorry," the bartender was moved to add, after a close scrutinization of his expression.

In Wonderland—

Axford's face said clearly that destiny had failed him. Axford's hand motioned the bartender about his business. Then it pulled on Cheesebread's ear until the former gnome extracted himself from the one-way conversation he was in with the brown lady.

"We're deep in," Axford's mouth said into his ear.

"What?" slurred Cheesebread. He was drunk on serious brownness, with extensive proportions.

"A pile of horse manure."

"What?"

"Has hit the windmill."

"What?"

"We're in trouble."

"Oh. *That.*" Cheesebread, even in his advanced state of muzzy-mindedness, knew that word. His whole body sagged and Axford thought he began to cry, though of course it was difficult to tell, what with the beard and the hair.

Axford turned to face forward again. He inspected the view from across the rim of his pint. The girl who was sitting next to him and fiddling with the peanut bowl snatched it from his hand.

"That's *mine*," she said.

"Beg y'r pardon," said Axford, wiping froth from his mouth and frowning. "They all look alike."

He wasn't going to give her an argument, but she made one anyway.

"And even if it *is* yours, it's rude of you not to offer it to me, you know. I need it more than you do."

"Why's that?" said Axford in serious doubt.

"Because," she said slowly, as though this was something he should know already, "Death is after me."

"Death."

"Death. Capital D."

"Never met the fellow," said Axford. He rubbed his chin ruminatively. "What's he look like?"

"He's a robe. Not just has one. I mean, he *is* a robe. And a cowl. And a sickle and a horse. You can't miss him."

"Hmm."

"He's never been after *you. You* don't know what it's like."

"Perfectly true," said Axford, lifting his other pint in an attempt to escape the superfluity of italics. "Perfectly true."

She snatched that one from him, too. "What. Did. I just. Say," she said through her teeth, like a third-form teacher with a particularly dense student.

Axford relinquished it without a fight. After she had swallowed it she seemed slightly less irritable.

"Sorry," she said. "I'm not always like this."

"Of course not," said Axford, who didn't believe her.

"It's just that, when death is after you— you tend to get a little, well, flustered."

"Really."

The girl slumped over the bar, chin on her folded arms, and heaved a sigh that even from several feet away made the bartender's toupee undulate. "Are you a good listener?"

"What?"

"Oh, never mind."

"Why is, er, Death after you?"

"Oh. He says I'm beautiful. The most beautiful girl, he said, that he's ever seen."

This put her in rather a different light. Axford looked her over curiously. She did the same to him.

"Do you think I'm beautiful?"

"No," said Axford truthfully. "I think the stars are beautiful," he offered.

"Which stars?"

"What?"

"Which stars?"

"No stars in particular," said Axford, confused.

"Oh," she said, and hiccoughed. "I thought you were talking about Johnny Depp, or David Beckham, or— somebody."

Axford let this go for a moment, and then was forced to say, "What?" because he still didn't understand it.

"Or possibly," said the girl, with an odd light in her eye, "Marlon Brando. No, he's dead, isn't he. Though I don't see what difference that makes to *me* at the moment. I'd go with anybody who could save me from him."

"From Marlon Brando?"

"*No*, stupid, from Death."

"What's so bad about death?" asked Axford, who was beginning to be genuinely interested despite himself. "I mean, you humans are always talking about a fate *worse* than death—"

"Yes," she said gloomily, "but nobody's ever faced a fate worse than death, *from* Death. At least I think I'm the only one. I could be wrong." She looked thoughtful. "He's probably had lots of girlfriends, actually, the dirty rotten cad."

"I don't know what you're talking about," said Axford politely, "but you could come with me if you like. There's no death where I'm from."

"What, really? No Death where you're— where *are* you from?"

He took a deep breath. "Wonderland," he said.

"Aaaaahhhh," she said, slowly, and exhaled. "For a minute I thought you were serious. For a minute I thought you were from Mars."

"Mars?"

"Well. Space, anyway. The stars, you know. All your talk confused me." She dropped her head onto the bar with a solid thunk. "My stomach is sloshing," she said indistinctly.

"So is mine," said Axford, "and I haven't even drunk anything yet."

She sat up quickly, looked at him with a compassionate expression. "Now *that* is a bad state of affairs. You poor, poor thing. I will buy you a drink." She rapped on the counter with her fist, and produced a hollow sound and a hurt hand. "Bartender, bring my friend a drink," she ordered imperiously. The last time Axford had heard anyone say anything imperiously was the Queen, and he twitched in anticipatory dread.

The bartender had been happily occupied in a corner with his own glass, and he did not react favorably to this. He gave the girl a glare and stomped over to slam a glass down so hard it sloshed most of the liquid over the sides.

Axford reached for it anyway, but the girl intercepted him and five minutes later, the glass joined the line of others on the bar in front of her. She looked up with a watery smile and saw the bartender waiting with his hand out.

"Oh dear," she said, and started the business of slapping her pockets hopefully. "I've run out of money, it seems. Been here for several hours, you know. Do I get any discounts for that? The sour expression on your face seems to suggest not. Do you mind?" she asked Axford.

"Not at all," he replied gallantly, and began digging through his own pockets.

"After all, I was getting the drink for *you*."

"A good point, good point." He was still looking.

"So pay the man," said the girl, looking worried. "I don't want to have to wash dishes for the rest of my natural life. Or unnatural one, either. Both."

"I will, I will." Axford saw his billfold peeking out of Cheesebread's pocket. He clicked his tongue at the gnome's treachery and lifted it back. "Here you are, my—" He choked involuntarily on the word "good" and just said "man," instead to finish up.

"Hey, wait a minute," said the bartender, with dawning irritation, "I just saw you take that from that man there."

"Yes, yes, but it was mine to begin with," Axford assured him. "Well, not actually mine, as such, but I stole it first."

The bartender, all his heretofore latent ethics suddenly rearing their ugly heads, started blustering. He was the point of tapping ineffectually at Cheesebread, who was still absorbed in the woman next to him (she was still ignoring him but had been steadily pocketing his money), when Axford took it upon himself to offer the solution that had done such wonders with Soul Train back home.

"After all," he said, "it's not whose money it *is*, it's whose money it *becomes*, right?" And he held the billfold out towards the bartender with a smile.

Who grunted. "Not as long as I only get a set salary," he said, and threw them out.

The horse kept running away from him.

Death, who had ruminated seriously on the idea of a first name, and decided that he might as well go with the one that Killjoy had boasted of (Fredreiche Felix Killjoy, that is), was rather bewildered. The horse didn't seem inclined to run away all together— he merely sidled ten steps forwards whenever Death tried to creep up on him from behind. And when Death turned to go, the horse followed, still true to his master, albeit at a distance.

Death couldn't understand this.

He had failed to take into account how old the horse was. The horse had enough trouble carrying himself most of the time— carrying a death who weighed no more than his robes and his sickle was as much as he could bear. Carrying a Death who weighed 168 pounds, *plus* robes and sickle, was out of the question, and the horse, with the intelligence and fatalism common to such creatures, knew it.

But Death hadn't quite got this figured out, and now he took a running jump at the horse, and missed completely as the horse bolted several feet away.

Death lay on the ground. He rolled over on his back so he wasn't breathing dirt (which he had discovered, was not good for humans) and rested for a moment. This was the fourth time this had happened. The robe was getting dirtier and dirtier, the dust of centuries overwhelmed by the mud of the here and now. There was probably a telling metaphor in there somewhere, but he would have had to dig for it.

This living thing was different than he'd thought. He'd assumed it would be easy, but if the average human underwent this without just plain and simple giving up, obviously he'd underestimated them. The average human was not, of course, likely to find themselves in this situation, but he didn't know that.

Of course, this was probably just a bad bit, and he'd get over it before too long. There were quite a few things that he had to look forwards to yet, vast worlds of experience that stretched out in front of him, waiting for him to arrive. Death thought this over, and smiled his fiendish smile.

"I've had a hard day," he announced to the horse, standing up. "You may go now. I may go too," he added, and sloughed off to a pub, with the horse coming slowly along behind.

"My name is Axford Barrel. I'm a man on a mission."

"Lovely to meet," she said airily, swept her arms around, got distracted, found her place again, and finished, "you. My name is Breca Sigh."

"How wonderful for you," said Axford politely.

"Yes, isn't it."

"Not really."

"What's your mission, then?"

"I'm looking for Alice. But they tell me she's dead."

"Alice?"

"Alice."

Breca nodded deeply, her hair loosening and falling into her face, where she watched the trailing strands as they shifted moodily from side to side. She looked up at Axford slowly and opened her mouth, a look of intense concentration on her face as though she was struggling for wisdom in a benighted world, when in fact she was merely struggling to hold onto the liquor inside her and follow the train of the conversation. She paused, mouth open, then said, quickly, "Who are you looking for again?"

"Alice." Axford sighed and rubbed his hand over his face.

"Alice in Wonderland."

"Yes."

"Why are you here, then? Why aren't you in Wonderland?"

"I *was* in Wonderland," Axford explained patiently. "I *started* in Wonderland, you see, but Alice left there and came *here.*"

"How do you know she came *here,* exactly?" asked Breca, with rather more sharpness than he would have expected from her at this point.

"Well," said Axford, and had to think about it. "Well. This is where the rabbit hole came out, you see."

"I see," she said, nodding deeply with a profundity that was presently alien to her nature. "I see. What?"

"We came up the rabbit hole,' said Axford, and grinned. "Quite a unique experience."

"And you came to look for someone who's obviously been dead for years, if she ever were even real. Someone from a book."

"Book?" said Axford, startled.

"Yes. A book. Wonderland was in a book. You must be from a book, too. What *did* that man put in his beer?"

Axford overlooked the bit about the book, but the enormity of everything else hit him suddenly.

"Dead," said Axford. "Dead, dead, dead, dead, dead, dead."

"I should say so," said Breca, and did. "Dead, dead, dead, dead, dead, dead."

"But it's only been nine years!"

"Ah, in Wonderland, *maybe,* but not here," said Breca. "Not here. It's obvious, isn't it? If you and I had a race, I'd win before you'd even started." She giggled to herself at her incomparable wit, then shook her head at her own frivolity.

Axford lifted his head and looked at her suddenly.

'You could come," he said.

"Beg your pardon," said Breca.

They dodged around each other for a bit as Axford tried to get a look at her profile and she tried to keep facing him.

"I could tell them you're her," he said. "There's a statue of her in the city, I've seen it. Your nose— your nose— it's exactly like, see."

"Exactly like what?"

"You're perfect, see. They wouldn't know the difference, see, all the people who knew Alice are in the Museum now and you needn't go see them, see. Sure! You'd be great!" He was getting quite excited about it now.

Breca kept preternaturally still for a moment, and thought. "You want me," she said, "to go with you," she said, "to Wonderland," she said, speaking as though each word was part of a separate thought and needed to be compartmentalized or there would be lots of unplanned word babies.

"Uh-huh."

"But the man in the pub wanted me to go with him."

"Huh?"

"That's *two* propositions I've had thus far. That's impressive if I do say so myself. Unless you count the one from Death."

"But I *am* the man from the pub," he tried to convince her. She wasn't paying attention.

"Would you count the one from Death? He didn't want to marry me, or couldn't, or something. I think it seems quite likely he was just going to put me on a pedestal, like a trophy wife, except without the wife part. Frankly," she said confidentially, "I have my doubts about his character."

"Do you?"

"Do I what?" She stumbled, and he caught and held her. "Propositions," she said, waving her arms. "Propositions. What am I bid. What am I bid. Going once— going twice— going!" She held very still and peered into his eyes as though trying to get a message to his soul. "Sold to the man with the terrible hair. Provided he agrees to get it cut."

"I agree," he said, laughing. "I promise I agree with anything you say. Will you come with me, Breca?"

She looked at him squintily. She appeared to be confused.

"Come with you where?"

"Back home."

"Home?"

"Home. Wonderland."

"Oh," she said. "That."

"Yes, that."

"Absolutely. Why didn't you say that in the first place?'

She straightened up and wrapped her arms around his shoulders and looked thoughtfully into his face. "I say, are you all right? Your face looks a little squishy." She prodded it back into shape.

"Too much beer," said Axford, and laughed, because he hadn't actually had any. "Too much you."

"Did I mention," said Breca, "that Death is after me?"

"Funnily enough," he said, "I'll take my chances." Death was something that happened to other people.

Death was happening to a tree across the pub, behind which he was hiding. He watched them stumble off together with a mournful expression on his face.

"Oh, Breca, Breca," he said quietly, leaning his cheek against the rough bark as the tree began to wilt, the leaves draining of color and beginning to slip off the stems. "When will you learn? When will you ever learn?"

But he was thirsty, and he went to find out the effects of alcohol on a human body.

When he wanted them, he knew where to find them.

Chapter Eight

Breca lay beneath an old apple tree, and the first thing she saw when she opened her eyes was a multitude of blossoms. She thought this was peculiar, as it was far too late, or possibly too early, for apple trees to be blooming. She may have been wrong about that, but the peculiarity was almost welcome regardless.

"Where am I?" she said. "In Wonderland already?"

Then she laughed, because of course that man at the pub yesterday had been stark raving mad, despite his beautiful strange eyes. And his nose. Breca was invariably attracted to noses, and Axford's was fine.

Axford.

Funny name, that. Axford Barrel. But then, *her* name was Breca Sigh, and she supposed she wasn't in a position to judge.

She shook her head, and sat up to look for Axford the madman, smiling in anticipation. She was unexpectedly and enormously disappointed to find that he wasn't there.

She sighed, let her smile drift into nonexistence, and leaned back against the tree. She tried to remember exactly how last night had ended.

Pub—beer—another beer—Axford's beer— getting thrown out—Axford was a thief, she remembered suddenly, with the slightly dizzy swelling feeling that comes from returning mind function, a bit like riding out a storm on a water bed, but the fact that the madman was a crook didn't bother her unduly, for some reason— her promise to come with him to Wonderland— staggering off into the dark—

And—

And then he had led her down a long and winding road. She had stumbled and he picked her up and carried her for what was probably a very long way, since there hadn't been any apple trees nearby, but hadn't seemed long at all. His arms were rock hard with muscle, she told herself serenely, not quite certain whether this was true or not. He'd said something fuzzy about how nice it was to be big enough to carry her. She hadn't quite understood it, because of how tired she'd been, but she'd smiled at him anyway and tried to kiss his neck.

Then he'd laid her on the soft grass underneath the tree, moved the rock that had initially been underneath her head. He'd sat beside her, smoothed her hair and touched her cheek with the tip of his finger, and leaned close and said—

And said. What had he said? She frowned in concentration. The water bed flurried under her.

He'd said—

Ah, yes.

He'd leaned close and breathed, "I'll be back in time for breakfast," in her ear.

And then he'd left.

"Which probably explains why I still have my clothes on," she said aloud, and with unabashed complacently. If Death couldn't resist her, what chance had a poor mortal like Axford Barrel? None at all.

There came a genteel cough from the other side of the tree, and a nasal, but genteel, voice said, "Well, er, I should hope so."

Breca twisted her head round the other side and saw a rabbit. She squeaked slightly like a frightened mouse, and blinked. No, not a rabbit, either. A man with a flat nose and reddish eyes and pale fur— or rather, hair, pale hair. He wrinkled his nose and quivered at her. He had whiskers, too, long thin sparse whiskers, three on either side of that flat nose, like a cat.

No, like a rabbit.

"Well, er, sorry to startle you, miss," he said.

Breca yawned. "Listen, love, Death's been after me since yesterday. I'm past being startled. *Quite* past."

"Well you did squeak rather—"

Breca waved this away. "I had that squeak all planned out. I was going to do it anyway. Honestly, you didn't startle me. I don't startle easily. Any more."

"Ah, good," said the man, relieved. "That'll make things easier."

Breca sat forward so she could see him better. There were ants on the tree, anyway, and one of them had just decided to investigate her ear. She flicked it away from her.

"So, you know Axford, then?" she said.

"Axford?" said the man. "Er— small chap, offensively orange hair in lots of little braids, upwardly mobile nose?"

"Yes," said Breca, pleased especially to have her opinion of Axford's nose upheld by a presumably unbiased source. "That's him."

"Never seen him before in my life," said the man, nervously, fidgeting his paws— or rather hands, she corrected herself— together. He frowned. "My name is Geoffrey, by the way."

"How nice for you."

"I expect you're a bit surprised at meeting a life-size rabbit."

"Why should I be? Aren't all rabbits life-sized? Other than dead ones, I should say, obviously."

Geoffrey thought about this and then coughed apologetically. "Yes, yes, er, sorry. Larger than life, I should have said."

"Ah, well, that I wouldn't know. I've never met a larger-than-life size rabbit."

Geoffrey blinked at her, looking closely for any evidence of startlement on her part. "Well. Well. Er. Well. *I* am a rabbit."

Breca smiled at him. "Oh! I didn't realize that's what you meant, see. Yes, you do look quite like a rabbit. How smart of you, to point that out before you get made fun of. Humble, too."

"Yes," said Geoffrey, nodding frantically. "I expect you think that I'm a bit— oh, abnormal, shall we say?"

"Well, I don't know about that." Breca yawned again, ostentatiously. "You'd be surprised what passes for normal around here. At least, I *think* you'd be surprised. You may not be. It's an estimation based on my own way of looking at things, you see. If I didn't already know, and somebody told me, *I* would certainly be surprised. Some of the things I've heard about—"

"Well, yes, er," said the man. "But a six foot tall white rabbit, I mean, come on, don't you think?" He smiled nervously. "Er," he added.

Breca brightened considerably. "Ah, yes, I saw that movie a long time ago. I liked it."

"Er—"

"I don't quite remember what it was called."

"Er—"

"Hartley or Herman. Something beginning with H."

"Er."

"And at any rate it was six foot three."

"Er—"

"And a half. I remember that." Breca sat back again, obliviously crushing half a dozen ants against her shirt. "Yes, I remember that very clearly."

"Er."

Axford's dog, whom Breca had barely noticed the night before, came out of nowhere and licked her hand, then started to crawl up into her lap. Suddenly it stopped and scratched viciously at its ear.

"Hello, little puppy," crooned Breca, and petted it. It looked at her with crossed eyes.

"Funny," she remarked to Geoffrey, "I wouldn't of thought that Axford would be the type to have a little squirty dog like this."

The dog backed off from her hand and cocked its head at her.

"It wants to know what you mean by squirty," said Geoffrey gloomily.

Breca laughed. "How do you know?"

"That dog and I go way back," said Geoffrey, grimly. "It talks, you know."

Breca had been concentrating on the conversation, and she hadn't heard Axford coming up behind her. Now, he cleared his throat and she turned and smiled.

"You cut your hair!" she said.

"I did," said Axford, and bowed. "As per our deal."

"You look great!" said Breca. Axford cleared his throat again, this time in embarrassment, and tapped his foot on the ground to distract himself from blushing. His hair had been unbraided, washed, and chopped. It now sat on top of his head rather attentively, like a trained seal.

"I found an all-night barbershop," he said. "They had quite a time getting all the braids out. That's only natural, considering they've been there more than twenty years. The braids, not the barbers. They— the braids again— were a present from my grandfather when I became a man at age five. We reach maturity early in our family, you know. Hi, Geoffrey," he finished up, waving a little. Geoffrey murmured something unintelligent. "Hi, Comfit," Axford said. To Breca, he explained, "That's Comfit, the Queen's Shi'Tzu. It talks."

"A talking Shi'Tzu," said Breca, who didn't believe him any more than she'd believed Geoffrey when he tried to tell her the same thing, but decided it was politic to be polite and feign interest with Axford, "how fascinating."

"Look what else I found at the barbershop," said Axford, and jerked a thumb over his shoulder. Behind him stood a man and a woman, hand in hand with peaceful faces.

"Ah, Rune!" exclaimed Geoffrey, jovially for no particular reason.

"This is Eldritch Rune, you know," said Axford to Breca.

"How nice to meet you," she said, with a brief flash of unwelcoming teeth. "Axford, this is getting to be like a hippie commune from the Sixties."

"And this," said Axford, oblivious, "is the girl he wouldn't leave behind. John."

"Remy," Remy corrected him.

"John," Axford corrected himself. "I thought John was a funny sort of name."

"Ah, I've been meaning to talk to you about that," said Rune.

"What, the name?"

"No— well, sort of. Mostly just her in general." Rune took him by the arm, flashing an apologetic grin at the new girl, and tugged him away.

Behind them, Breca smiled at Remy and Remy smiled back.

"Not very nice to go off and talk secretly," Breca offered.

"No," said Remy, "it's not."

Rune glanced back at them to judge that the distance was sufficient, and turned to Axford with a serious expression. "Now, look, about Remy."

"Not about her name."

"Not her first one. No."

"Then what? Her nose?"

"Shut up."

"Ah, just her in general."

"Right."

"Right. Shoot." Axford folded his arms and did a marvelous imitation of deep interest.

"Listen." Rune waited a few minutes, eyeing him closely, to see if Axford would comply with his wishes. There was a pause in the conversation that indicated adequately that yes, Axford was. Rune took a deep breath. "Axford, what does destiny mean to you?"

Axford thought this over. "Fame, fortune, and success," he said finally.

"Fantastic. Does that have anything to do with what Noughts and Crosses told you before we came here?"

"Well, the success part, maybe—"

"You don't sound very sure," said Rune with a frown.

"The rest is just wishful thinking, you see." Axford gave vent to the reminiscent grin that wishful thinking always brought up in him. Wishful thinking had been, on the whole, much kinder to him than reality, over the years.

"Is it?"

"Listen, Rune," said Axford, shaking his head regretfully, "I hate to tell you this, but that girl out there? She's *not* Alice. Not *really* Alice. Her name is Breca Sigh."

"Breca what?"

"Sigh."

"Sigh?"

"As in the sound you make."

"As in the sound you make?" Rune put a hand to his chin and pondered.

"Yes. Stop repeating me. My point is, I'm going to have to pass her off as Alice. Because otherwise, if I don't bring Alice back, my destiny will go unfulfilled, Wonderland will forever be oppressed, the price of beer will just keep going up, and all sorts of things could happen that aren't very nice. So it may not work, this Breca instead of Alice. But I have to try. I can't go home empty-handed. The Twins were mistaken somehow, Rune, I don't know if their Intuition failed them or if they read it wrong. But Alice has been dead for a long time. The Twins were *wrong*."

Axford paused for breath and Rune said, in a voice so quiet Axford had to lean close to hear:

"Guess what?"

"What?" whispered Axford.

"You from around here?" said Remy, off to the left of them. She was making conversation and never dreamed that the smallish, oddish looking girl would have taken her up on it.

"No, I got kind of dropped off on my way somewhere else," said Breca. "I'm being chased by Death, you see, and then I met Axford in a pub and woke up with my clothes still on and, well, here we are."

The conversation, thankfully, stalled somewhat after that.

"The Twins told me," said Rune, still in his low tone, "what would happen once we got here. They told me I could be happy again if I found the right one. They even told me where she was. Sort of."

"How do you mean?" asked Axford sharply.

"They told me to look for the Barbershop Quartet."

"What?" said Axford, confusedly.

"Well, I went into the barbershop. Guess what I found?"

"What?" said Axford again, curiously.

Rune leaned very close and said, in a voice heavy with portent, "I found Lenin, Max Artney, Harrison, and Starkey."

"What?" said Axford again, blankly this time.

"Those are almost the names of a group of musicians from Alice's world."

"*Almost?*"

"Yeah, almost, not quite. Four of them. They work in a barbershop. Barbershop Quartet, see?"

"I see," said Axford, although he didn't, really. "Or nearly, anyway. I think perhaps you are the only one who could have made that kind of connection, though."

Rune shrugged, as though this was the sort of compliment he could do without. "I'm the only one with this destiny."

"I suppose that makes sense. But what's the deal with the musicians?"

"Oh, nothing important. I read a bit about them at a record store. Their music was very gear, fab, groovy, and far out. All those things."

"Wow," said Axford, solemnly considering the ramifications, if any, of this. "A mysterious language. What does it mean?"

"I don't know. But my point is, I found the girl didn't I?"

"Yeah, you found her alright," Axford agreed. "But what does she think of you? Does she know where you're from, or what you really look like, or anything?"

"N-n-no—" said the Fiendish Thingie, gazing into the middle distance with a worried look as he considered the ramifications, if any, of that.

"Well," said Axford, putting his hands on his hips and raising his eyebrows, "don't you think you'd better tell her?"

Remy was somewhat alarmed at the expression on Rune's face as he emerged from the underbrush into the clearing. He looked pale and worried and grievous. She didn't like it, even despite the nose that dominated it.

She stepped forward, and held her hands out towards him. "Is something wrong?"

Rune flashed her an uneasy smile, and said, "Can I speak with you a moment?"

Here it comes, she thought, as she let him lead her to one side. The big send-off. The let down. The pink slip. The quirked eyebrow that said *You didn't really think I meant it, did you?* The, as it were, goodbye.

She'd seen it all, and it broke her heart every time. What worried her the most was that she'd run out of the fixative it took to put herself back together.

"First of all," he began, "let me tell you how much I appreciate the time we've spent together. Even though it wasn't very *much* time, from the moment you took the scissors to my hair I felt that you were someone very special."

"That," she said, peering anxiously at him, "is a very bad sign."

"Eh?" he said, but shook his head before she could explain, as though it didn't matter, and went on. "Now, I'm going to tell you something that you're going to have a great deal of trouble believing." He took a deep breath. "I'm not from Hampton Downs after all, as I told you I was. I—I'm from Wonderland."

Remy regarded him with polite eyes. He waited for a reaction, for he'd expected more than that, but getting none he went on.

"Wonderland," he repeated. "You know, that place you go when you fall down the rabbit hole? That—" he gestured, "is the rabbit hole. I climbed up it, and came out here. We were searching for Alice, it's a long story, but— look, before I left, these two sisters, named Noughts and Crosses? They're able to see into the future, it's a kind of intuition. They told me I would find complete happiness with someone from Alice's world. You."

A slow smile started the trek across Remy's face.

"Really?" she said.

"Really," said Rune, with an answering smile matching Remy's, step for step. "I can stay here with you and we'll be happy. If you want it."

"If I *want* it?" she repeated incredulously. "Of course I want it!"

She threw her arms around his neck and buried her face in his shoulder.

"Wait a minute, wait a minute, wait a minute," said Rune, disengaging her grasp before he was choked to death. "There's something else. There's something— more."

"How could there be more?" Remy asked, muffledly and delirious with happiness.

"Well, I'm not— exactly— human."

She looked up at him, the smile fading slightly. "What?"

"I'm, well— I'm what's known in Wonderland as a Fiendish Thingie."

"A— a Fiendish—"

"Thingie. Yes. But— 'Fiendish' for short."

"Wow," she said. "That's. Surreal."

"Yes," he agreed.

"But what does that mean? What's the difference?"

"Well, in my normal state—" he said, and hesitated for a moment, then closed his eyes in concentration. The change was gradual. His ears grew, his nose grew, a finger grew on his left hand. After a minute he opened his eyes.

"In my natural state, I look like this," he said unhappily, not daring to meet her gaze.

Remy took a quick, deep breath, and a look at his profile.

"Do you think I *care*?" she said, so happy her voice ended in a squeak.

Fiendish Thingies have no upper lip. They are very difficult to kiss for this reason. Almost impossible, in fact.

Almost.

"Well," said Axford from not too far away, "looks like that's settled."

He turned to look at Breca, who hadn't been paying the least attention to the tender scene taking place in the bushes. She was instead frowning thoughtfully at Comfit.

"I swear," she said, "that dog just mouthed something at me."

"Of course," said Geoffrey patiently, folding his arms. "It's a talking dog."

Breca turned a suspicious glare on him. "So you keep saying."

"Hark," said Axford theatrically, "a happy Fiendish Thingie approacheth."

Rune came up to them, nearly dancing. He had a great big grin on his face. "I can't stay long," he said. "We're going to pick out a wedding ring."

"What for?" Axford wanted to know.

Rune cast a thoughtful glance at Breca, who was casting a thoughtful glance at Axford. "You stay here in Alice's world much longer, you may find out," he said.

Axford followed his gaze, met Breca's, and frowned.

"At any rate," said Rune, "perhaps the Sisters were right about destiny, eh?"

"What do you mean?"

"Hey listen, son, if it can happen to me it can happen to you." Rune clapped Axford on the shoulder in a misguidedly father-like manner, and Axford glanced at him shrewdly.

"Which? Destiny or wedding rings?"

"What makes you think the two are separate?"

Axford thought. "You know, I'm not entirely sure what you're talking about."

"At this point, it hardly matters, because you're going to find out soon enough one way or the other. I've got to be going. Give my regards to Wonderland, hey?"

Rune turned and stretched his legs jauntily down the path.

"You know," said Breca, tapping her fingertips on her lower lip, "I'm almost certain his nose wasn't quite that big before."

"Oh, well," said Axford archly, "you know how things are."

"Hmmph," said Breca thoughtfully, and suddenly smiled. "He must have been telling lies, huh?"

"No," said Axford. "Truths, actually."

"Truths?" said Breca. The concept was a new one.

"Truths," said Axford, and looked at her with a new light in his eye. She straightened up and gave him her full attention. "Speaking of which— are you ready to go to Wonderland, be brave and a savior and all that— in short, rescue everybody's peace of mind from almost certain obliteration or something along those lines?"

Breca thought about this. "How many people live in your Wonderland, Axford? What's the population?"

"Oh, lots and lots."

"Lots and lots, hmm. And they only have one piece of mind between them. Dear me, what a sad state of affairs."

She laughed hysterically at her own joke for a few seconds, and Axford gave her a tolerant smile which meant, *If you tell any more bloody stupid jokes, I'll leave you here, Alice or no Alice, so help me God.*

"Alright, alright," said Breca, who could interpret tolerant smiles with an ease born of long practice. "We'll go to Wonderland— just as soon as you bring me some breakfast." She yawned and lay back, stretching her arms over her head and blinking rapidly. "Look here, Axford. Tell you what— while you're getting me breakfast, I'm going to go back to sleep. Don't think I'm lazy. It's just that I'm extremely tired and don't feel like moving at all, apart from breathing. I may not even bother to do that, depending on how tired I turn out to be. After all, I was up rather late last night, you know."

"Yes, I know," said Axford. "I was there." He cocked his head to one side and watched as she closed her eyes, folded her hands, and started her descent into sleep. A curious feeling came over him.

So Death had chosen her, forsaking all others—

Hmm.

He took two soft steps till he was at Breca's side. He bent over.

"Eggs?" he inquired gently into her ear.

"Two, please," she said, fighting to get the words out through a yawn and not entirely succeeding.

"Right enough," said Axford.

He smiled at her.

And then she was asleep.

Cheesebread the ex-gnome was fighting his way through the thick underbrush. He had been doing so for rather a long time, and was getting quite fed up, as only someone who has been incredibly small for most of his life can do.

"Where is it?" he snapped. "Have you found it?"

"I don't know," came the slow, strange voice of Dap-Hodil, somewhere off to his left. "The path seems to have gone."

"Perhaps it ran away when it heard you coming."

"Now, that wasn't very nice of you,' said Dap-Hodil, deeply and grievously offended, but Cheesebread had seen something slightly familiar in the way ivy was draped over a certain tree nearby, and was wading towards it.

"Aha!" he exclaimed a minute later. "I *know* we passed underneath that branch there on our way out, because I remember it smacked me in the face when you let it go."

"Ah yes," remembered Dap-Hodil.

"And you remarked at the time how strange it was that it didn't go right over my head as it normally would have done."

"And *you* remarked at the time, ow."

"Yes."

"Yes."

"So where's the path?"

They both looked around.

"Blimey. It really has gone."

Dap-Hodil stood up straight and breathed deeply, sniffing the air for any familiar scents, for anything that smelled of home. "That way is the rabbit hole," he said, pointing, and led on.

Upon reaching the tiny clearing that had been so recently the scene of the beginning of their adventures, however, they found that it was all grown up.

No, not *that* sort of grown up.

The clearing was full of plants, tangling wildly with each other in an impenetrable mess.

"Huh," said Dap-Hodil, "how strange." He walked around the tree underneath which Breca had so recently slept, and sniffed at it.

"Odd," said Cheesebread, frowning. "Almost as if the way between worlds is now closed, as if Axford's quest was successful, and Alice has been taken back, and — hey!" he cried, suddenly bouncing rapidly up and down.

"What?" said Dap-Hodil alertly.

"I've got an idea! Remember last night we were discussing what to do with our lives here, and I said that from the look of that thing called a 'movie theater' the entertainment business was undergoing a dry spell? Remember that?"

"You mean because of the marquee that said *Opening Today: All That Are Left After The Bomb Exploded And Killed Nearly Everybody Except Me* and that other one, er, *The Antiseptic Monk Battles The Angry Scotsman.*"

"That's right."

"Yeah, I remember that," said Dap-Hodil, doubtfully.

"Well, I tell you what we do. We write the story of our lives, see, and we make it into a movie! People will be lined up around the block! Think about it— all those people out there, coming to see us. We can be big time producers. We'll call it— we'll call it— *'Cheesebread and Dap-Hodil's Adventures in Alice's World.'* Huh? How about it?"

"*Cheesebread and Dap-Hodil's Adventures in Alice's World,*" repeated Dap-Hodil, thinking it over. He smiled. "Sounds good."

"Great!" said Cheesebread, casting a last fervent look around the former clearing. He paused and grew still. "Even so, it would have been nice if they would have said goodbye," he murmured to himself.

Dap-Hodil called to him at this point, and he hurried over to where his companion stood by a tree.

"Look," said Dap-Hodil.

Graven into the bark of the apple tree, carved by someone with a shaky grip on a knife and an even shakier grip on the idea of legible handwriting, was a single word.

Goodbye.

They looked at each other for a minute in silence.

Finally, the ex-wolf-man said, *"Cheesebread and Dap-Hodil's Adventures in Alice's World?"*

"Mmm."

"Wouldn't it be, well, more unusual if it was our adventures in

Wonderland? For instance, everything that happened to us before we were wrongfully incarcerated. We could exonerate our good names."

"Lie, you mean.

"Sure."

"Could be," said Cheesebread musingly.

"And why can't it be '*Dap-Hodil and Cheesebread's Adventures*?'"

"Well," said Cheesebread, "it isn't alphabetical, but I suppose that could work, too."

And the funny thing is, it did.

Chapter Nine

Breca was having strange dreams. Somewhere through them Axford walked, tall and bright and handsome, touching her heart each time he looked at her, albeit completely oblivious that he was doing so.

There was a face she didn't know mixed up in it all, too. The quiet eyes overlaid everything and made her shiver in her sleep. It was a handsome face but all she wanted was to run as far away from it as possible. She tried to run but something touched her cheek and a voice told her to shush.

The face was there again a moment later, wearing a cowl, surrounded by darkness. It reminded her of an uncle she'd been very fond of when she was little. He'd been run over by a tractor on her seventh birthday and died horribly.

What was dying *well*, then?

"Breca," said Death to her, speaking with those sad and terrible eyes as much as with that mournful mouth. "Why are you doing this to me?"

"Not to you," she said. "Not to you, not to you."

"Now, look, love," said Death, suddenly sounding awfully British, "I don't mind making myself a fool over you, just so long as I get to be a fool on a regular basis."

"Thanks," said Breca tartly, "in that case I think I'll go with Axford. At least he has some dignity."

The eyes froze at this and the ice spread over the face until the features could hardly be seen, unless she squinted and tried different angles, and then they suddenly bounded out at her in many facets, as though she looked at him through a diamond, vast and flawless. Then the ice melted and so did the cowl and the robe and Breca saw him as he had been the morning before, before he was Death. He was waking up in pajama bottoms and no shirt, his hair stuck up every which way. He pushed a wandering hand up, free of the bedclothes, quested the other side of the bed and found it empty and his eyes closed.

"*Please*, don't make me be as pathetic as that," said Death's voice in her ear.

"I think it's kind of sweet, actually," she said. "Has he lost his one and only, or not found her yet?"

"Neither," said Death. "He's so obnoxious, none of the girls at the pub will even let him buy them drinks."

"I think it's time to wake up now," said Breca firmly. She cast one last look at the sad-faced farmer, who opened one malicious blue eye and winked at her with it. A small smile quirked the corners of his mouth, and he dissolved into a million pieces.

Breca woke up and said, "Where's my eggs?" without thinking it through first.

Nobody answered her, and she saw that she was in a very different place from where she'd gone to sleep.

"Axford?" she said.

This got no answer.

"Eggs?" she hazarded.

Neither Axford nor her promised breakfast were in sight.

"Hullo?" said Breca, and sat up.

There was no one there. She was on some very soft grass, in between rows of red and yellow and white roses. Something about it touched a memory off in her and she said, "He *can't* have been telling the truth," desperately. But she wasn't sure she believed herself.

A curious little voice said behind her, "Kibble?"

She turned around. Comfit the Shi'Tzu sat there, staring at her with slightly crossed eyes. She remembered Geoffrey's attempts to convince her that the dog talked, and gave a derisive laugh, mostly for his benefit since she was not-quite-convinced that he must be hiding somewhere nearby.

"Oh look," she said, folding her arms and widening her eyes, "a talking Shi'Tzu, how interesting. Really, Geoffrey, just because you took a course in—" Suddenly the word for it deserted her. "—in learning to throw your voice."

What *was* it called, anyway?

She shook her head and patted the dog, who licked her hand obligingly, looked up at her and said, in a tiny clear voice, "I'd like some kibble, please."

Breca screamed and jumped, simultaneously to her feet and quite a ways away from the dog, who sat looking at her calmly.

Axford emerged from the middle of a wall and stared quizzically at her, too. She caught a glimpse of him and the screams abruptly died away, even though her mouth remained open.

"Carry on screaming, by all means," said Axford pleasantly.

"You— you're so— tiny!" She pushed herself back and huddled in a ball, looking at him in shock. "You're— half the man you were!"

"I had a mole removed."

"No, I mean it, Axford, you're quite small!"

Axford shrugged. "Really, that's hardly a cause for alarm. I've been short all my life."

"Not when I met you, you weren't!"

"Ah, well, must have been somebody else's life, then. What where you screaming for? Or at, rather?"

"It's demonized!" she shrieked, and pointed a quivering finger at Comfit.

This galvanized the little dog into action. It leapt to its tiny feet and started darting around in circles shouting, "Demon! What demon? Where demon? Demon!"

"It's not demonized," said Axford, fighting to swallow his laughter. "It's Comfit."

"I *know*, you *told* me, but why is it—"

"Talking? I told you that, too. Geoffrey told you that."

"Not—"

"Yes. Comfit the Queen's talking Shi'Tzu."

Comfit stopped darting around Axford's ankles, set his tiny furry rump down and gazed at Breca expectantly.

"How lovely," said Breca weakly.

"Kibble?" said Comfit hopefully.

Axford shook his head. "That's the trouble, you see," he said conversationally. "You might think it's a great thing, having a talking dog, but there's no point really. It's not worth the noise. All they talk is a load of mindless drivel about kibble, or the smell of things, or the bug they ate last week."

"Yes," said Breca, "yes, I can see that." She shook her head, and gripped it in both hands as it felt as though it would float away. "Why are you so small, Axford?"

"Oh, I'm always like this."

"You weren't when I went to sleep," she objected.

He grinned. "That is perfectly true. But you fail to take into account the fact that when you went to sleep, we were," he pointed at her, "in your world."

She swallowed. "And what world are we in now?"

He placed both his hands flat, palms down, on his small chest.

"Mine," he said with a self-satisfied smile. She hadn't noticed before how sharp and canine his teeth were.

Breca was not a tall girl at all, but Axford was nevertheless a good foot and a half shorter than her. She looked down and he looked up and she shook her head in disbelief.

"You'll have to remember, while you're here, that you aren't Breca Sigh— you're Alice. The same Alice who came here and played croquet with the flamingos. The same Alice who talked to the strangest creatures Wonderland holds. The same Alice who revitalized our souvenir industry. The same Alice who walked these very garden paths. The same Alice who—"

"Alright, alright," said Breca. "I get the picture." She glared at him. "Are you *sure* this is Wonderland?"

"Positive. On my word of honor."

"That's very reassuring."

"We dropped you down the rabbit hole in your sleep. But we dropped Geoffrey down first, so you had a nice soft landing."

"*Very* reassuring," she repeated. "You know, despite your sudden shrinking and the talking dog, I do have marked difficulty believing you."

"That's too bad," said Axford sincerely. "Because it's very rare I tell the truth. I like it to be appreciated when I do."

Breca shouted, "Ventriloquism!" at the top of her voice, and when Axford looked at her questioningly she only shrugged and stared about her at the garden in which she stood. She shook her head.

"You keep doing that," said Axford. "Why?"

"Because it's far too surreal. It's like a cartoon. The colors are brighter, the grass is softer, the—" She frowned at the ground. "The ants are waving to me as they go merrily by. One would almost think—"

"Yes," said Axford. "One would."

"But it's so unbe*liev*able!"

"Think of it like this," said the raven suddenly, perching on Axford's shoulder with a flutter of his dusky wings. "Two days ago, you would never have believed that Death could show up at your door and offer to take you with him. Never mind all the marriage stuff, you have to admit that it's incredible that he should even ask your opinion on the subject instead of just dragging you off by your hair." Breca winced. "But according to you, that's exactly what happened yesterday. Now, you were always told Wonderland was in a book, right? Now, just because you were told something your entire life by everyone you know doesn't mean it's true."

Breca stared at him. "That," she said, "is an extraordinarily lucid bird."

"You can understand him?" said Axford disbelievingly.

"Of course I can understand him!"

Axford and the raven exchanged glances.

"Here," said the raven, "have mine."

"Oh, thanks," said Axford, "here's mine."

"Thank you," said the raven politely, and then they both turned and looked at Breca again, tilting their heads to one side.

"But he was speaking Raven English!" pointed out Axford.

"So? What's the difference?"

"They're two separate languages. That's quite a big difference!"

"But I didn't even hear an accent," said Breca reasonably.

"I don't do accents," objected the raven. Breca squinted at him for a moment, then turned back to Axford.

"Why, what are you speaking now?"

"Cockney English."

"And the bird speaks Raven English?"

"Yes," said Axford, looking pleased that she'd caught on so quickly.

"Well, there you have it," said Breca airily, "just two different types of the same thing. Back home, we have American English and— well— English English. But we understand both. Some of the time," she amended.

Axford and the raven exchanged glances again.

"Here," said the raven, "take yours back, it doesn't work for me."

"And yours," said Axford, "doesn't match my mental furniture."

"Thank you," said the raven curtly.

"Thank *you*," said Axford, more curtly.

"Would you *stop* doing that?" said Breca.

"Listen, Breca," said Axford, coming forward to reach up and take her hand. He tugged on it till she sat down so he could pretend to be taller than her. Axford thought this was very polite of her.

"Now listen," he said again, "it's very important that the people here really believe you to be Alice. I could explain it—"

"Please do," said Breca.

Axford heaved a sigh and did so. Breca listened with a frown as the story of Wonderland's need of saving was unfolded.

"As far as I can remember from the book, Wonderland was kind of— crazy, wasn't it?"

"Yes," said Axford immediately. "Yes, crazy."

"Really?"

"Yeah. But a lot happier. Everything's gone downhill now." He frowned. "Quite a lot down hill. About as downhill as is possible to get."

The raven, who'd picked up quite a lot of geography while in Alice's world, said, "From the tip of Mount Everest to the bottom of the ocean, that's *my* rough estimate."

"I'm beginning to get your point," said Breca. "But is it still crazy?"

Axford started to exchange glances with the raven again, but Breca said, "Ah, ah!" and they stopped.

"Oh yes," he said. "Quite mad."

"Mad as a hatter, eh?" said Breca, again pleased, overmuch and without reason, with her own wit. "He was my favorite."

"Oh, no," said Axford. "I think you'll find that the Hatter is considerably more sane than most of the others."

"Really?" said Breca again.

"No," said the raven, covering Axford's face with one of his wings. "He's making a good bit of this up, you see. Wonderland has merely, since Alice left, become bloody boring."

Breca looked outraged at Axford.

"But you said—"

"Ah, yes, I know," said Axford, hopping nervously from one foot to the other. "But I did tell you I was a liar. Why didn't you believe me?"

"And you want me to be Alice so it can go back to being all nice and insane as a stick insect again, right?"

"Yes," said the raven.

"But I'm not Alice. So why should it work?"

"It'll be like a sugar pill," said Axford. "Wonderland will think its been given its medicine when in fact it's been given Breca."

"And you expect that to work?"

Axford shuffled his feet and put his hands behind his back, looking recalcitrant. "There's no telling, to be honest."

"Honest," said Breca with a certain bitterness, "hah."

"Breca," said Axford, sitting in her lap. "Breca, please give this a go. You've come all this way, you might as well."

"Oh, get off me."

Axford latched his hands around her neck. "Not till you agree."

"Axford, get off."

"Say you will."

"Axford."

"Say you will."

Breca struggled to her feet— Axford locked his legs around her waist and held on.

"Let go!"

"Come on."

"You're clingier than my ten-year-old nephew, do you know that?"

"Say you will."

"Heavier, too," said Breca, staggering.

Axford looked into her eyes. "Breca. I will do anything you ask me to, *anything*, if you promise to pretend to be Alice."

"Including letting go?"

"Yes, I am prepared to make even that sacrifice."

"Fine then," said Alice with infinite exasperation, folding her arms and not yet truly playing the part.

"Boy," said the raven. "That was quick."

Widden and the jailer sat together with their legs up in the air.

"Really," they said to everyone who passed, "it's a lot more comfortable than it looks."

"And anyway it's a diplomatic position," opined the jailer, squinting upwards to where he was framing the clouds with his feet. This time in the stocks had given him a welcome vacation from the dark cells he normally habituated.

"Excuse me?" said Widden.

"Oh, it's not important."

"Well, my interpretation of your peculiar remark," began Widden thoughtfully, nonetheless, "is that it is inherently politic to make yourself appear extremely silly before everyone else, so that pity is taken on your shabby attempts at sanity, and you don't have to work at being likeable. It seems that the only creatures who don't realize this are those who make their careers as politicians. One can only assume that, for these few, looking extremely silly comes naturally. There, what do you think?"

The jailer nodded in enthusiastic admiration.

"Well, what is your take on this? Is that what you meant?"

"Oh, no," said the jailer. "Oh, no, no, no. *I* just thought it sounded rather distinguished."

"Well," said Widden. "There is nothing in this world so misguided as voicing your opinions just because *you* think that they sound *distinguished*. That's how politicians are made, baby."

"What have you got against politicians, anyway?"

"Well, the Queen is one."

"No! Really?"

"Yeah. Pure and simple."

"How awful for her."

"How awful for *us*. Can you imagine, the country being run by a politician?" Widden shook his head. "It's no wonder things are so bad. People are falling apart, families are getting group rates on psychological examinations, a bunch of convicts have gone missing right from the cells, earthquakes and other unheard-of disasters, our armies invading other lands, and the cabbage has been almost *entirely* de-valued. So much economic stress, too."

"How can you de-value a cabbage?" questioned the jailer.

"I understand it to be quite difficult," said Widden thoughtfully. "It should have taken advice from the lettuce and quit while it was ahead."

"On the other hand," contributed the jailer, "it is probably a good thing that we're living in a monarchy. If we had the vote, I mean, that young swine that was talking about running for office could actually have got in. Say what you will about the Queen, having pigs in the castle is not advisable."

"Could have been worse."

"How?"

"That cloud formation! Did you listen to him? His platform was pure rubbish. All that talk about more rain for the masses."

"Really? I kind of liked it."

"Are you kidding me? Complete airhead."

"Well, no argument there."

They lay there, silent, for a while.

"I still don't understand, though, why the Queen put us in the stocks backwards."

The jailer said, "I don't understand why she put us in the stocks at all."

"Well, I don't know about you," said Widden, "but I was keeping a small blue hamster under my bed, and she had me arrested for being unmanly."

"What's unmanly about a blue hamster?"

"Search me," offered Widden.

"Thanks, I don't think I will." The jailer patted him gratefully. "I mean, I could understand if it was a *pink* hamster—"

"I still miss the little guy," said Widden, beginning to sniff.

"Or maybe pale yellow— with little flowers—"

"Hammy, I called him. Hammy the Hamster."

"Or lavender, maybe—"

"I can't believe she flushed him down the toilet."

"She *what*?"

"Yes. There he was, even after she bopped him on the head, trying to swim. He was always afraid of water—" Widden's tears overflowed finally, and the jailer began to cry silently, too, in sympathy. "Scrabbling with his little paws—"

"Oh, that's awful!"

"I know! He just went right down! And she made me watch!"

"Oh, that's *awful*!" said the jailer again.

They subsided in to choking, gasping sobs. After a while, Widden raised his head a little and said, "Oh, look, here comes Alice."

Chapter Ten

Alice had floated in, holding Axford's left hand and Geoffrey's right, stepping delicately on bare feet. Her dress (*"What do I do about that?" Breca had asked. "Look, all I've got is this robe, because Death got me out of the bath, you know, and it's getting kind of ragged anyway." "Never mind, we'll find something," said Axford cheerfully, "take off your clothes."*) floated around her ankles. Her hair (*"Right, what about that?" asked Breca. "My hair is red and straight. That can't be right." Axford had grinned very broadly and produced, from behind his back, a wig.*) cascaded down her shoulders and back in a tumultuous waterfall of golden sunlight.

Her eyes (*"Well?" said Breca. "Well, we can't do much about that, really," admitted Axford.*) were still her own, but they had taken on a light she hadn't had previously— a light of endless, insatiable curiosity.

"Curiouser," she said, and her voice was a bit higher, slightly less resonant, "and curiouser."

"Don't do that," said Axford between his teeth.

"Do what?" she said, and she was, for once, for real, all innocence.

"You're supposed to be grown up a bit now," he said. "A nineteen-year-old would know better."

"But a fifteen-year-old wouldn't," she said sweetly, and Geoffrey (*"I don't like the idea of this," he said, "cheating the whole Kingdom." "You've no choice," said Axford wearily, having been through this numerous times, "because if we aren't successful, guess who goes back in his cage for all eternity?" A phrase which had a particular sting in Wonderland.*) chuckled nervously.

The crowd had appeared as if from thin air. They watched and cheered and cried as Alice walked among them, with her oh-so-pleasant smile that turned a little frightened when something akin to Dap-Hodil picked her up and gave her a ferocious hug.

Axford was trying to steer her towards the castle entrance, but was having some trouble as she was continually distracted and appropriated. There was the Fiendish Thingie couple who wanted her blessing on their children— the caterpillar who claimed to be related to the one she'd met the first time, and who immediately got into a fist-fight with another caterpillar who claimed the same thing— the snake who threw itself at her feet and begged forgiveness for some unspecified wrong— the enormous shirtless man with the Alice tattoos on his arms and chest who said, "I'm your number one fan!" as tears streamed down his face— there were, everywhere, the faces of the creatures of Wonderland, looking to her to give them something better.

There was the tiny little girl, no more than half an inch taller than Axford, who was accompanied by a large cat. She came through the crowd almost unnoticed, touched Breca's hand, said, in a voice only she could hear, "The Twins welcome you. Noughts and Crosses send their greetings. The Sisters of Intuition wish everything you do to be blessed."

And then she was gone.

"What did she say?" asked Axford, leaning close and upwards. Breca looked down at him.

"You couldn't hear her?"

"No."

Breca thought about this. "Then," she said, "I don't think you were meant to."

No matter how many times he asked her after, she wouldn't tell him any more than that.

They came in this way to the castle at last. The Queen herself stood at the great doors, accompanied by her Watchdogs who, alert at the presence of so many creatures, twined around each other with hungry eyes; she waiting with her cold, proud head held high, waiting without the slightest bit of welcome on her face, though there was a hand-lettered sign in front of her that said, for anyone who wished to read it, ROYAL WELCOMING COMMITTEE.

Breca approached and stood before the Queen, with her hands clasped in front of her, looking winsome and sweet and— ever so slightly— nervous.

"Ahhhh," said the Queen, dramatically, "Alice."

Breca said nothing.

"We certainly welcome you to Wonderland," said the Queen, raising her hand and gesturing at nothing in particular. She was trying hard to roll her Ws and was finding it difficult, as had many pompous speakers over the years.

Breca said nothing.

"Presumably this visit will bring great joy and prosperity," said the Queen, raising and lowering her eyebrows rapidly, as though signaling by semaphore, "if you know what I mean."

Breca still said nothing, but appeared to be deep in thought.

"I," said the Queen, "am the Queen. The highest power in the country."

The raven snorted. He'd heard Widden and the jailer talking, and having learned that the Queen was in fact a politician, felt quite betrayed.

Breca's lips moved silently, as though she were practicing what she was going to say before she said it. Finally her voice became audible.

"Thank you so much," she said carefully. "Been quite a long time, hasn't it?"

As this wasn't the most interesting statement in the world to start out with, the Queen turned her attention to Axford, who stood in a vaguely proprietary manner at Breca's elbow. She frowned slightly and, though his knees felt weak, he grinned back.

"Ah, Mr. Barrel," she said. "You came back."

"Yes," agreed Axford. "Must be one in the eye for you, mustn't it?"

"Quite," she said. "Where are the others?"

"They decided to stay in Alice's world. Most of them didn't even bother helping me look for Alice," he couldn't resist adding.

"So you, Geoffrey, and the raven came back, leaving the others."

"Yes. Well, and the dog."

"Abandoning," said the Queen, savoring the word, "a*band*oning the others."

Axford bristled. "Now look," he said, "it was completely the other way around, you know. *They* abandoned *us* is what I mean to say."

"Still," said the Queen, "it is *you* who are here, safely home again, and not them."

"That's because they ran away!"

"Hmm, so you say," said the Queen, by which it was quite evident that she didn't believe him.

"I *am* telling the truth!"

"I don't believe you."

"But I *am*!"

"And I don't care!"

"Listen," said Breca coolly, "can we, like, not argue, is that groovy with everyone?"

Everyone turned and looked at her with their mouths open slightly.

"Because like, I love peace, man, you know? All this yelling really brings me down." Breca nodded her head till her curls started a slow, waving motion.

"I think," said Axford in some haste, "that Alice would like a little nap. The trip's been— rather— strenuous— for her."

"Yeah," said Breca, as she was being led off, "it's been a really heavy trip, man. Peace out, man."

Axford led her through the halls, the sentries standing straight as they approached and then sagging with faint sighs of relief as they went past.

What do you think you are doing? said Axford loudly, though inside his head. He was practicing for when they were by themselves. *WHAT do you THINK you are DOING?*

"The chambers for Alice?" he asked a nearby guard.

"Why not say Alice's chambers?" asked Breca, cast a glance at the startled guard, and added for effect, "Groovy, baby."

"Because it sounds— funny," snapped Axford back.

"Yes, it does sound kind of vaguely naughty, doesn't it?" she agreed whole-heartedly.

"Er, that way," said the guard, pointing.

"Thank you," said Axford, so quickly and sharply that it sounded like an insult.

"Are you hip, man?" said Breca to the guard. Axford grabbed her hand and pulled her down the corridor in the indicated direction. "Save the whales!" she shouted over her shoulder.

They finally achieved the rooms set aside for Alice (complete with a large sign that said ALICE'S CHAMBERS, which was rather hard to miss) and Axford pushed her in, then slammed the door and banged his head on it a few times.

"What do you think you're *doing*?" he yelled at her, but Breca had fallen onto the bed and was trying to muffle her laughter in the pillows.

"I don't know," she said between fits of giggles. "Everyone's always on about how *Alice in Wonderland* is just about drug culture. I don't agree with that, I just extrapolated, I suppose. It seemed appropriate."

She was overcome by laughter once more. Axford watched her and felt most of his anger slipping away, though he still didn't exactly feel like joining in the merriment.

"Breca," he said when she had quieted enough for him to be heard, "you did promise, you know."

"I know. And I *will* be Alice. I will."

"How can I be sure?"

"You can't," she said, hiccoughing. "But that's part of the fun, see."

"Not very fun."

"No, not very."

They sat for a while in a warm and companionable silence, Axford absentmindedly tracing Breca's wayward strands of hair with the tip of his finger.

"You'd better stay here for a bit," he said finally. "There's a big royal dinner tonight and I'd prefer that you make absolutely sure you won't—"

"Be a hippie again? A flower girl, a child of peace and love?" She grinned at him.

"I suppose. Whatever it was you were doing. Just— you know— rest. Prepare yourself. You think we're all strange here, I know, but— really, you have no idea *how* strange. Alright?"

Breca smiled at him. "Okay," she said.

He patted her hand, half-jumped, half-fell off the bed, and went out the door, closing it firmly behind him.

Breca lay on her back, looking up and telling herself twisted nursery rhymes.

There was an old lady who lived in a shoe
Of knots there were lots, and so she was blue
She had lots of children, but not lots of loot
And so when she died she gave them the boot.

"Little Boy Blue fell asleep in the barn
Dreaming of knitting with needles and yarn
Cats in the cradle, dogs do a jig
He awoke in the muck with four cows and a pig.

Far above her the ceiling stretched, tall and white and dim. After a while it blurred and her eyes closed. She wasn't able to think clearly anyway and she might as well sleep—

Mary had sheep, and John had a cow.
Each to their own, a curtsey or bow
They met in the garden, sat down for a meal
John had roast lamb, and Mary had veal.

Death was there, in her dreams. He was sleeping, too. After a while (as she watched him sleep and was peaceful somehow, watching the rise and fall of his breath, still not believing for a minute that he could be mortal, could be human) he opened his eyes and looked at her.

"It's not a bad place, where I come from, you know," he said. "Takes a bit of getting used to— but it's quite nice, actually."

"Yes, well, I've heard quite a lot about it. I've had it pounded into me since I was little, it being exactly the kind of thing you threaten small unruly children with. Flames and everlasting torture and all that."

"Breca," said Death. He shook his head. "There is no Hell, you know, not of that sort. If there is, it starts when you're born, not when you die."

"I say that is a very cynical attitude for someone who hasn't even had to experience life."

He looked amused. "Well, I've experienced it now. The parts of it that go on in pubs, anyway."

"That hardly counts."

"On the contrary, it seems to be, to some people, the absolute last word."

"Then what happens?"

"After death? After me? There is nothing, after me. Sleep."

"But I don't want that," protested Breca.

"Well, it'd be a little different for you."

"How?"

Death sat up, rubbed sleep out of his eyes, and yawned.

"Well, *I'd* be there."

She woke as she was still saying, over and over at him, "*No no no no no no—*" She shifted in her bed restlessly, turned onto her side and looked directly into Death's face as he lay peacefully sleeping beside her. He woke up as she turned to him and stared at her with his terrible eyes.

This brought on a screaming fit which woke her up all the way. She sat up and tried to stop shivering. The room seemed to have gotten a lot colder all of a sudden, and the covers on the bed were thin and ineffectual.

Dream within a dream, she thought. It sounded a lot nicer than it actually was. Well, she wished it would just go happen to someone else. Someone who wasn't having nightmares.

She lay back and looked at the ceiling and wondered if it went on forever. Perhaps she could only watch it till it went out of her sight, and then she'd never reach it again.

Axford thought he was being very brave, marching (well, shuffling) back to the Great Hall, wherein waited the Queen with her fiery eyes. Most likely the first thing that she would do, now that he had outlasted his usefulness, would be to throw him back into the cell—it'd be just like her to do it, too, he thought darkly; she'd probably really enjoy it.

He walked down the cold, echoing corridors, thought he heard some snickering going on behind his back, turned and strode over to the wall and attacked it with fists and feet.

"No, that was me actually," said the Wolf, stepping out of the darkness into the light.

Axford tried to swallow his tongue but was prevented from it by the fact that it was still attached to the floor of his mouth. He placed a hand on his heart, gulped, shifted his weight.

"Did I scare you?" inquired the Wolf.

"Not at all. Nice try," said Axford, albeit a little stiffly.

The Wolf looked at him. "I don't know about you, little man," he said. "I don't know why you got sent to look for Alice instead of me."

"Perhaps," suggested Axford delicately, "because the Queen knew I wouldn't eat Alice when I found her."

The Wolf was fat and was middle-aged. He had a face like a loan shark, or a fourth-rate lawyer on the make. But he had teeth that could have shown a rack of knives a thing or two about edges, and he ran a greenish tongue over them now as he looked thoughtfully at Axford, who flinched.

"Don't look at me like that," he said. "You make me feel so judged."

"The Queen is waiting for you," the Wolf informed him. "She doesn't like to wait, you know."

"Don't know about it, actually," said Axford brightly. "She's been waiting for years for you to start becoming something useful. I think she's probably figuring by now that she got the bad end of the deal when you walked in. It would help if you could, you know, start brushing your teeth, cut your hair, lose that spare tire maybe. Have you tried dieting?" Then he sighed sharply and shook his head as the Wolf growled low in his throat. "I don't know why I do that, I just let my big mouth run on before I manage to think about it. And always, *always*, it happens at the worst of times! I mean, look at you! You're five times bigger than me at least. And yes, you are old and fat and ugly, but hey, ugly can be a positive *boon* to someone who earns his living as a lackey. No— sorry— didn't meant that, didn't mean that. Obviously you have a much more prestigious position than a lackey. Henchman, maybe. But what I'm trying to say is, the only advantages I might have over you, apart from my brains and good looks, in a combat position, that is, a *combat* position, the only advantages I have are that I'm smaller and quicker so I can run away—"

And he did.

He arrived, nearly breathless, in the Great Hall a few minutes later, and stopped cold in surprise at the amount of people there, waiting for him. There were representatives of every species in Wonderland there, all holding their breaths in hushed silence, and waiting, anticipating—

Well. Not him, he had to admit. Axford Barrel they could see on the street any given day, if they cared to look down. No.

They were waiting for Alice.

The Queen confirmed this opinion when he made his way to her side of the room. There was a chair over there, made especially for someone his size. Furthermore it had a large sign on it that said AXFORD BARREL, HERO on it in ornate letters. He examined it with interest and appreciation. It was, he had to admit, a nice gesture.

"Where is Alice," said the Queen. She had mastered, quite some time ago, the art of asking questions without the proper punctuation.

Axford watched the pull of her facial muscles with rather disgusted delight. He had never seen anyone try to grin charmingly whilst speaking out of one side of their mouth.

"She's having a lie down."

"But they," said the Queen, making fierce little jerking motions with her hands at the assembly, "are waiting."

"They've waited a long time," said Axford. "They can handle a bit more. Alice was tired, she can't properly work her wonders if she's tired. That's what you want from her, isn't it? Wonders?"

The Queen sighed through her teeth, producing a whistle. Comfit, who'd been snoring at her feet, woke up at this. Looking up, its eyes lighted on Axford. It scrambled to its feet, leapt into his lap, and started licking his face.

Axford fended it off.

"Why is it that dogs are always overjoyed to see you, even if you've only been gone fifteen minutes?"

Comfit closed its mouth momentarily and looked confused, which was not, for a dog with that face, difficult. "I don't know, really," it said. "Must just be our nature. Kibble?"

"No," said Axford firmly.

"I didn't really expect it," said the dog resignedly, and licked his face some more.

The entertainment at the banquet was not to be missed. It was largely comprised of one of the descendants of the Mad Hatter, along with descendants of the March Hare and the Dormouse (not that the originals couldn't have done it themselves, but they had long ago sought to retire from a life in the public eye and were, as a result, permanently kept in the Museum commemorating their part in Wonderland's history, where they were gawked at from ten to five every week day), being dragged in, chained, leashed, and grinning frantically, and made to repeat all the poems that had ever been written in Wonderland, which were many.

"A donkey and a duck one day did chance their paths to merge
"In vain the duck did turn away to cause them to diverge
"The donkey crossed in front of him and with his mouth a-lather
"Challenged the bird to take back what he'd said about his father.

"The duck just blinked. Though he knew there had been a dispute
"Between the two of them (they both were quite of ill repute)
"He said amazed, 'Be calm there, friend! And don't be in a bother,
"'Not one single word did I say about your father!'

"The donkey was amazed by this. 'What was it, then, you said?'
"The duck replied, 'You misheard. Not your father, but instead
"'Your mother did I comment on. I wish you'd let it pass!
"'Nothing but the truth spoke I: I said she was an ass!'

"Enraged by this fowl language, the donkey bucked and brayed
"The duck was startled into flight, feeling quite dismayed.
"The ass was so surprised at this he hardly drew a breath!
"In bewilderment he trampled the duck unto his death.

"It seemed that once again, violence would rule the day
"The donkey stopped and stared in horror at the duck paté
"The authorities at last informed, an action was suggested
"And without much more ado, the donkey was arrested.

"When police came to interview the witness of this crime
"Which the two antagonists did perpetrate in rhyme
"'I must admit,' said the watching hen, with a humble cluck,
"'When it comes to it, I'd rather be a donkey than a duck!'"

The entertainment left something to be desired. Rapidity seemed the chief concern, and the trio managed to get through all the poetry surprisingly quickly. Then there was nothing but a dead, uncomfortable silence in the room: the sound of everyone waiting.

Geoffrey the rabbit, fully returned to his natural form and yet not looking any more at ease for it, was seated next to the Queen. He plucked at her sleeve till she turned to him impatiently. He jumped at the look on her face; or, perhaps, just at her face.

Poor idiot, thought Axford. *You'd think he'd have gotten used to it by now.*

"Um, I was just thinking," said the rabbit, "that maybe, since Alice, er, can't be here for the moment, if you would perhaps oblige the people by, er, making a speech?" Under the weight of the Queen's glare he had wilted and shrunk until his head hovered just above his knees, and his arms were placed protectively around his head.

"And what," said the Queen, in daggers, "do you suggest I say?"

"Er, you could— er, introduce the man who saved us all—er—" Obviously, this was not the right way to put things, and the rabbit could tell by the silence he was getting. He dropped his ears over his head, and looked abjectly miserable.

"Are you referring to *that*?" said the Queen, pointing at Axford.

"Er," said the rabbit. "Yes."

"*That*?" thundered the Queen, inexplicably, it seemed, giving him a chance to withdraw.

"Er," said the rabbit.

"That *midget*, that beardless *dwarf*, that orange-headed little *twit*, you have the gall suggest that *he* is the one that saved us? I'm amazed you were able to refer to him as a *man*!"

"Er," said the rabbit, shooting nervous glances at the assembly, who was watching all this with the keen eyes of a populace deprived of entertainment, "shh!"

"*Shh?*" repeated the Queen in tones of shock. "*Shh*? You tell *me* to shh?!"

"Your Majesty," said the Wolf smoothly, who had appeared as out of nowhere as usual, "perhaps you would care to distract the subjects from the fact that Alice is not actually *here* at the moment?"

The Queen considered this, hissed an annoyed breath out through her teeth, and stood.

"Subjects," she said, "lend me your ears. On second thought," she added when Axford sniggered, "just listen to me. No, *listen*," she demanded as an anticipatory murmur ran through the crowd. "Shut up. Pay attention to me. I am your queen, after all. Look, shut up, please!"

"That," said Axford, "was the most unconvincing *please* I've ever heard."

"Right, now," said the Queen loudly, over in the general din that remained, "I'm going to make a speech. And, er, quite a good one, too. Er— what do I say?" she asked the Wolf quickly.

"Hype it up," suggested her henchman. "Build so much anticipation that they can't help but be disappointed."

"Well, uh, it's going to be good. Great, that is. The best speech you've ever heard in your life. Never will the likes of it be heard again. And if you disagree you'll have me to answer to. Got that?" She turned back to the Wolf. "And what now?"

"Start with a general overview of the effect this great speech will have on their lives, then move on to the stories they'll tell their children about it," he advised.

"Right," said the Queen, and did her worst. Axford watched the fidgeting and restless crowd with amusement and asked the Wolf, quietly, "Whose side are you on, after all?"

The Wolf shrugged. "What do I know about speech-writing? I'm just a Wolf."

Fifteen minutes later, the Queen said, "And now to begin—"

Alice walked into the room.

The old magic spread in waves from the door as she entered. She stood among the denizens of Wonderland, smiling gently, looking slightly confused, slightly still-childish, standing on the verge of the wonder of adulthood with the wonder of childhood looking over her shoulder— *so much* Alice. Axford thought, with a little thrill of secrecy, that if he hadn't known it was Breca, he would be just like the rest of them now, standing there dumbstruck and deliriously happy, eyes wide and mouth agape. Certainly he'd never thought that she was such a good actress. Certainly he'd never thought—

He closed his mouth hurriedly and wiped at his chin.

This didn't seem to be quite enough, so he coughed and cleared his throat loudly, too. The Wolf, who stood behind him with one hand on the back of his chair, gave him a curious look.

"Ah, hullo everyone," said Breca with a wave. "So nice to see you again. I feel much better for my nap, you know, a little less like a deranged hippie escapee from a Rolling Stones concert. Tell me, has anyone here seen a short little man with deceptively blue eyes?" She stood and played with her hair at them.

There was a moment in which the world held its breath, and it was filled by the sound of every creature in the room letting go of theirs, in a collective rush of sighs that raced towards the young woman standing just inside the door, mussing her hair like a breeze. There was satisfaction in that sound.

Applause broke out, thunderous applause from every pair of hands in the room, as though she were a particularly difficult high wire act.

"Yes," said the Queen, beaming jealously with teeth half-gritted. "Yes, yes. Same old Alice." The crowd continued to roar. "I said, I said— shut up! Please!"

"I take it back," said Axford, "*that's* the most unconvincing please I've ever heard."

The Queen tried to shout them down, aurally beating them into submission, but no one was paying her the least bit of attention. "I said, same old— SAME OLD ALICE I SAID!"

Except, of course, that it wasn't. But she wasn't to know. Even when Comfit had tried to tell her earlier, she had said, "Oh, shut up," and trod on its paw.

The Queen watched as the crowd clustered around Alice, watching her with adoring eyes, reaching out with reverent fingers to touch her curls, the sleeve of her dress, the curve of her cheek. Breca, caught in something totally new to her—adulation— got lost somewhere in it and laughed and held out her arms to every single strange inhuman being. The Queen felt something prick her under the fingernails, something she was quite familiar with and had felt on a regular, almost daily, basis since she was three years old.

Envy, it was. Jealousy.

Oooh, she thought. *This can't be good.* She didn't bother to pursue this thought and figure who, exactly, it wouldn't be good for.

Breca looked over the heads of the creatures surrounding her (with difficulty, as many of them were well over eight feet tall) and found Axford's eyes. They were bright and sharp with repressed mirth, and the singular feeling of being in on the secret.

She knew how he felt. Elated. Successful. Happy. She blew him a kiss, which he dodged without much trouble, still smiling.

She followed it up with a wink, and he caught it right in the heart.

Chapter Eleven

J ealousy.

The Queen stood on a balcony and brushed her hair.

Tangle.

Smooth it. Attack it till it's gone. Kill it with kindness and a hairbrush.

Tangle.

Blast it.

She saw Widden, newly released from the stocks, crossing the courtyard below her with unsteady steps, and threw the brush at him. It hit him squarely on the skull and he gave a brief, surprised glance at the blue sky above and then collapsed.

The Queen snorted in satisfaction and selected a new brush from the rack of them at her side. She'd had one installed every ten feet in her chambers, when she'd become Queen.

That was another thing, though, she thought, looking up at the sky in distaste. It was blue now. It was blue all the time. It was the same color as Alice's dress.

She really, really hated it.

You used to get proper weather, five days ago, before Alice came back. Lots of storms. Feet and feet of snow. Flash-floods, trees blown over, drains overflowing and stars obliterated. The Queen frowned. All this sun— It made her rather annoyed.

And what *was* it with the dancing in the streets? It was constant. She didn't mind it on occasion, but this was *all the time*. Somebody had even written a song about it. She didn't like it at all.

She didn't get it. She'd wanted Alice back for one purpose— to get the Kingdom back on track. She hadn't counted on all this *happiness*.

She liked that even less than anything else.

The Queen, had she ever fathomed the idea of staying outside for longer than the duration of a summer banquet in her honor, and had the custom of spending a week in a grimy little tent with a campfire outside been common in Wonderland, would not have been a happy camper.

Breca sat with her feet up, lounging on the window seat, looking out at the blueness.

"What's with the blue?" she called.

Everyone wore sky blue, the same color as the dress Axford had stolen for her. It seemed to be some kind of tribute.

"What's with the weather?"

The sky this morning was blue, blue, blue, just as it had been every other morning she'd been here. Breca was getting a bit bored with it, something she shared with the Queen, albeit somewhat less dramatically. It wasn't that Breca minded good weather, of course, but she wouldn't have minded a little rain now and then, either. Just to liven things up.

"What's with the dancing?"

She peered out the windowpanes. Geoffrey the rabbit had overcome his natural shyness, and was leading everyone in a step he called (Breca shuddered) the Hop.

"Which question do you want answered first?" inquired Axford, shoving at her feet to make room. She obliged, lifting them up, then replacing them in his lap once he had settled himself. He looked at them in consternation, looked at her and smiled weakly, patted her feet gingerly. "It doesn't really matter, the answer to each one is the same."

"In that case," said Breca, and thought. "Answer the second one. I'm really concerned about the weather."

"Simple," said Axford, with a wide grin. "Wonderland is happy."

"Happy?" she said. She lifted her feet from his lap, shifted to her knees and looked down at the tumult. "Happy?" she repeated. "What's the deal with that? Why are they happy? What's to be happy about? What's happy *for*, anyway? What's another word for happy, Axford? Axford, why is this working?"

"*Giddy* is a good one," said Axford slowly, leaning forward and staring at Geoffrey's exhibition. "And, well, *silly* is a word which applies in this case. As for why it's working—"

He paused and looked at her. She looked confused and rather miserable.

"You're homesick?" he said.

"No." She shook her head. "That's not really it."

It was, though.

Axford nodded, and went on. "I think it's working because all we needed was someone from Alice's world, and Breca'll do. In a pinch."

"Don't even think about it."

"What?"

"Pinching."

"What?"

"Breca'll *do*? Well, I must say, *that's* encouraging," she said. "And I'm being sarcastic. I mean the exact opposite."

"Well, I didn't mean to insult you."

"Yes, you bloody well did! Why else would you say something like that? That was your express purpose! Insulting! Insultation!"

"No, see, I just—"

"I just don't like being lied to."

"I—" said Axford, and gave up. He felt quite confused.

"Yes, I am homesick," said Breca, and sniffed.

"Oh, don't start, please don't!" said Axford urgently, and patted at her shoulder.

"I'm not starting *anything*." Breca wiped at her eyes. "So you think all you needed was a— a representative from our world."

"Yeah, that's what I think. It's logical, anyway. And things are definitely going back to normal."

"Normal?" she enquired, somewhat drily.

"Yes, well, normal for us. Yesterday, as a matter of fact, a team of badgers won a football game against Dalyas the Giant, and the flowers staged a showing of *Madame Butterfly*." He grinned, so obviously fond of his homeland that she couldn't help but think of her own. "So what do you think? Breca in Wonderland, pretty flash, eh?"

She sniffed again, and smiled. "I think 'Representative in Wonderland' is more to the point."

"Oh, why not get personal?" Axford spread his arms wide.

She smiled, leaned over quickly and kissed him just below the ear. "Thank you, Mister Barrell."

"No problem." He patted her arm. "What, er, what was for, what you just did?"

"Um, appreciation, I guess. You don't have kissing here, then?"

"Only on alternate Tuesdays."

"Axford." She shook her head at him, like a worried school guidance counselor with a student whose ambition in life is Queen of England. "You should get out more."

"Maybe I should."

She turned away from him and looked out the window once again. "Why is the Queen always brushing her hair?"

"Oh, just a deal she made."

"What kind of deal?"

"Well, there's lots of theories, but the truth is funner still." Axford sat up, eagerly. "It's kind of a protection for the country. If she's good for us, all's well. If not, a time trap is set up. I love time traps. So timey. So trappy. In this case, when she goes to sleep, poison starts at the ends of her hair and creeps up towards her head. If it reaches her, something unspecified and vague happens and she's removed from her position. Probably the government men come get her and put her safely away in the Museum with the rest of the relics. On the other hand, if she brushes it out in time, she's safe, till next bedtime anyway. It's sort of a game."

"Yes, well, you in Wonderland have a truly remarkable sense of humor," said Breca, shaking her head. "How do you know about this arrangement, anyway?"

He shrugged. "Common knowledge, on the street, along with all the theories. And I spend a lot of time on the street."

"So if she had been good for the country, kept it happy, she'd not be playing a game with her life? Oh— no—" she held up her hands as Axford prepared to interrupt, "that's right, I forgot, no death in Wonderland. Right. That is why I'm here, after all."

Axford, surprised, pouted. "I thought you came because I wanted you to. Because you wanted to help."

"Ah, yes, that too, but self-preservation's pretty high on my list, you see. Funny about the Queen sending you to look for me, though. Or Alice, rather. I mean, she'd have to figure that if I brought happiness and prosperity back to Wonderland, I'd be quite popular. I mean, there's a movement now for crowning *me* Queen." Breca leaned out the window, and clasped her hands together, pensively. "If I were her, I'd be rather jealous—"

The Queen was getting rather jealous. There was a very good-looking young man in her sitting room, tall and thin with serious brows that indicated he did lots of puzzled frowning over the many things he couldn't figure out. He'd come to meet with Alice, he said, twinkling indiscriminately at the maid. He'd been sent by his uncle, the White King, who lived two castles down. He'd really like to meet Alice. He was very pleased to see the Queen again, yes, hadn't seen her since that banquet thingie a year or so ago, wasn't that right? But he'd really, *really* appreciate seeing Alice now—

The maid had gone to call for her, not seeing the Queen's grimaces, which were intended to discourage her from doing so, but, to the casual observer, may simply have appeared to be the garlic prunes from lunch having trouble settling. At any rate the Prince, who had noticed the faces, became rather more adamant about seeing Alice. Soon. Alone, please. Please?

The Queen crossed her legs and glowered at the Prince, who tapped his fingers on the arm of his chair and grinned nervously.

"So," he said brightly, "how's the stamp collecting going?"

"It's butterflies," said the Queen, in a kind of dangerous monotone. "I collect butterflies. Queen Adam collects stamps, *I* collect butterflies."

"So sorry," said the Prince, with a quite pathetic attempt at a light-hearted laugh. "I knew that of course." The Prince, as brave and handsome as he undoubtedly was, was nevertheless nervous. It was rather too easy to picture the Queen stabbing pins through beautiful, frail, helpless creatures— he shuddered. "So how's the, er, butterfly collec—"

"Super," said the Queen, moving as few facial muscles as possible.

It was at this point, that Alice came in. Smiling brightly, as always, her small sturdy body wearing the blue flounced dress like a curse, and eyes that said *Who do I think I'm kidding? Oh, right. You.*

The Queen frowned at those eyes. She didn't like them at all. They were too intelligent, too knowing. Almost entirely unlike the young girl who had come curtseying and crying to visit nine years ago; of course it was to be expected that the girl would have grown up since then, but she'd hardly had time to develop *intelligence*. The Queen had been about a bit, and knew that young people's brains don't properly grow in until they're well into their thirties, and sometimes not even then.

The Prince liked Alice's eyes, though. He liked all of her. He shot to his feet and snapped a stiff little bow.

"MILADY," he said in capitals.

"Ah, Alice," said the Queen, expending great effort and being almost pleasant, "meet Prince Stoat."

"Your Highness-ness," said Alice, curtseying.

"Oh, please call me Stoat."

"Oh, alright— Stoat." She laughed very gently. It was an attractive laugh. Axford, listening from behind the door, had to stuff a fist in his mouth to keep from laughing himself. She was *good*. She was *perfect*. She'd only gotten better in the days of practice she'd had being Alice.

"Milady—"

"Oh, *Alice*, please," she said, and put her hands behind her back, rocked on her heels, and added, "Stoat," with a warm smile. These were all tricks she'd adopted simultaneously with her new persona— they really did make her look about sixteen or so, which was what, Axford had assured her, she was going for.

"Alice," said the Prince hesitantly, and blushed furiously. "Uh—"

Alice laughed her gentle laugh and tossed her hair.

"Uh—"

She looked up at him from under her dark eyelashes and bit her lower lip.

"Uh—" He grinned a sheepish, charming grin. "I've forgotten what I was going to say."

"Hah!' said the Queen. Alice laughed again.

"That's all right, I'm quite used to it."

("Lord, that was fun," she told Axford later. "I know I'm not pretty, but you have no idea how invigorating it is to pretend to be, and pull it off.")

"Well, I feel like a fool, coming all this way and forgetting—"

("Oh, you're quite pretty," said Axford absently, looking at her feet. He'd become quite attached to them, actually.)

"Oh, I'm sure it will come back to you. Just talk to me about something else and it'll drift right back to your mind. Consciousness is like that sometimes— gets away from you just when you're driving straight for it. Or do I mean conciseness? No, it could hardly be that— I talk far too much to even give that a passing thought."

("Do you think I'm the prettiest girl in the world?" she asked, and "No," said Axford automatically, flicking at her toenail.)

"Well, I, er," said Stoat, stuttering slightly, "thank you so much, for being so understanding—"

("Well, Death does," she said huffily, tucking her feet underneath her. "Yes, and if it's appreciation you want you can go right back up the rabbit hole and find him," said Axford irritably, deprived of his foot fetish.)

Alice smiled at Stoat. "Well, I *am* Alice, you know. That's just what I'm like."

("Oh, shut up, Axford," said Breca. "Haven't you got anything better to do?")

"Shall we go and have dinner?" suggested the Queen icily. "Or are you going to ask her to marry you right now?"

("No, I don't," said Axford. "I have two hobbies. One is you. The other is your feet. Sitting like that ruins your posture, you know.")

Prince Stoat said, "Oh!" and looked at Alice, abashed. "That's what I was sent to ask you. If you would consent to my attentions as a suitor. My father thinks it's a good political move. And, of course," he hastened to add, "I like you very much. At least, I think I do. I'm sure I will. Give me time to get to know you. I—uh— I don't have a lot of experience liking people, actually," he confessed. "It's just— I don't spend time with the most savory of people, you see, I mean, the average member of the royal family—"

"Oh, yes, I quite understand, and sympathize," Alice assured him. "But still, one can't choose one's friends, can one? Or is that said about love? Yes, that's it, one can't choose whom one loves. Though I've never actually agreed with that sentiment. Still, it's something to say, isn't it? At any rate, it doesn't matter. It can apply equally to friends. On occasion, that is. Tell me, Stoat, do you like ravioli? I've taught the cook to make it. It's an Alice's World specialty. Would you like some?"

"Yes, very much,' said the Prince politely. "It sounds very, um—"

"Well, I'm afraid the cook's ill today, so we won't be eating after all," interjected the Queen. The cook was ill, in fact, mostly because she'd gotten irritated with him and snuck some bad broccoli in his nightly vegetable pie.

"Ah well," said Alice, putting her arms behind her back. "Such is life, or so they tell me. And indeed my experience as well tells me that if something can go wrong, it most certainly will. We will have to come up with some other way to occupy our time. Take a turn with me about the garden?"

"Marvelous idea," said the Prince stoutly. Alice took possession of his arm and led him to the door, waving at the Queen as they went out, closing the door behind them.

Steam began to filter its way through the Queen's rarely-cleaned ears. Her eyes turned red and little horns began to grow up through her hair.

She was not enjoying Alice's visit. Not at all.

Death lay drinking out of a brown paper bag. A few homeless, scruffy men nodded at him and raised their eyebrows, broad hints to share the wealth among his kind.

"Push off," said Death politely.

They raised their eyebrows again.

"That's a broad hint," said one, "to share the wealth among your own kind."

"That means, gimme the bottle," said another, baring brown teeth in what was probably a smile.

"Only trouble being," said Death, holding a wobbling finger up at them, "that my kind are things such as war, famine, and pestilence, and they weren't as fascinated with the properties of beer as I am. Oh, God, I think I've become an alcoholic. How far gone am I, do you think?"

"Can you think straight?" asked the first.

"As a ruler."

"Do you giggle helplessly at very inappropriate occasions?" asked the second, almost wistfully.

Death thought. "What kind of inappropriate occasions?"

"Funerals of very close friends, that sort of thing."

"I don't have any friends," said Death, and paused a moment. "But I do attend a lot of funerals."

"What for?" asked the first, a bit suspiciously now. "You morbid or something?"

"No. I just like to gloat." It was a complete lie, of course, but Death felt that it fit this new persona he was trying build up, this humanity thing. He accompanied this revelation with a wide grin, showing every last one of his appropriated teeth.

The homeless men watched him with a certain amount of nervousness.

"Here, mate. You alright?"

"Never better," said Death brightly, and suddenly he sat ramrod straight and looked first into the sky, then down at the ground, then gave himself a slow, curious once-over from the ankles up.

"Hmm," he could be heard to mutter, "that's odd."

And then he was gone.

He appeared back in a flicker of time and space to grab his scythe, which he had forgotten, and to, with a grin, very carefully place the bottle he'd left behind as well.

The homeless men gazed in befuddlement at the empty space where he'd so recently been, and thought for a while.

"Reckon that guy was okay?" ventured the first.

"I dunno" said the second, slowly. "He looked kinda ill."

"Yeah," concurred the first. "He did, rather."

"As a matter of fact he looked like death."

"Yeah."

"Nice fella, though."

"What makes you say that?"

"Well, he left his bottle behind, didn't he?"

"Oh. Yeah."

They looked at each other, then at the bottle, which sat, in all apparent innocently, directly in between them, not looking in the least as if it had been Death's liquid lunch. They gazed at it with intensity, each one possessively, each one greedily, each one distrustful of the other.

They lunged at the same time, which had rather been the point of the experiment.

There was a peculiar sound, like three coconuts hitting together, and they sprawled in identical attitudes on the pavement.

It doesn't really matter, in the long run.

The bottle was empty, anyway.

"I'm jealous," announced the Queen, as the door slammed back against the wall. "I'm jealous and something had better bloody well happen bloody fast in order to make me not jealous anymore."

"Jealous,' repeated Comfit, musingly. "Why's that?"

"That bloody Alice," said the Queen, quietly, and then repeated it at the top of her voice.

Comfit tried to cover its ears with its paws, failing miserably. "Alice?"

"D'you know," said the Queen icily, "that those idiot peasants out there," she pointed a blood-red, three inch nail out the window, accidentally skewering a passing fly, "are actually talking about making her— a *queen!*"

"What an engaging idea," said the dog with warm approbation. "Breca is certainly a nice young woman."

The Queen was busy raging and appeared not to hear. She stomped up to the throne and kicked it several times, severely injuring her bare foot.

"Grrgkrrkgrrgkrrkgrrrrr!" she said.

Comfit was delighted.

"Your Majesty!" it said, "I had no idea you spoke Great Dane!"

"I didn't," she spat viciously. "Alice inspired me." She half stomped, half limped away from the throne to find something else to take her anger out on.

"Hope no one was planning on using that wall any time in the near future," said Comfit helpfully, "because, er, you kicked a rather large hole in it just now."

"Yes," said the Queen, using a tone of voice that, in our world, would be followed by, "Wanna make something of it?"

"With, er, with your foot."

"Yes," said the Queen again. "Wanna make something of it?"

"No, oh, no no no. Thank you. But, not at this particular time, no."

"Then shut up," she snapped. She sat down on the throne to think. It helped her cognitive process if she could feel superior to everyone else, and the throne was very high up off the ground. It hadn't been, before she was Queen, but she'd had it altered for the coronation and didn't see any reason to change it now, considering how much she liked heights.

Something was going to happen, she knew it. She'd made a deal— she *had* to remain Queen, just as long as she was alive. There was no way anything could change that, really. Unless–

She pushed that thought out of her mind and tried to focus. No, according to the terms of the deal there was certainly no way she could lose her position. Therefore, something had to happen in order to change things. She did not like the direction events were taking, and she thought it had better happen *soon*.

She thought hard about the endless variety of things this unknown event could take, and gave a slow, unpleasant smile.

Comfit watched her thoughtfully, for a moment, reflecting gently on how different humans were from dogs. If the Queen had actually been a dog, she would have just gone to Breca and bitten her, and then they probably would have made up and been friends after exchanging scents. It thought about this and then was understandably distracted by the bug that was hopping around by its paw.

Flea?

No, too big.

Beetle?

Maybe. More like a distant cousin—

Cockroach?

Huh.

Mmm.

Tasted pretty good, anyhow.

The Queen suddenly recaptured its attention by looking up abruptly and saying, sharply, "*What* did you call her?"

Chapter Twelve

"Erm, I was wondering," started Prince Stoat.

Breca looked up dreamily from the water. "Hmm?" she said.

"Was wondering." The young man sat up attentively and leaned towards her slightly, a preparatory smile on his face.

"Oh. Terrific. No better place for it." She went back to watching the water as the boat slipped smoothly through it. The Prince had arms bulging with muscles that were purely ornamental, which meant he was completely unequipped to deal with actually rowing, so she'd taken charge of the oars when they'd started out. Now she was tired, but pleasantly so, and content to watch the scenery without actually paying the least attention to her companion.

There were trees on the banks, every so often, and they were the biggest trees she had ever seen. She smiled at them absentmindedly and was profoundly startled when one of them smiled back.

It was a big smile.

Lots of teeth.

The sun bounced and gleamed off them as though they were a bank of bay windows.

Breca jumped to her feet, rocking the boat dangerously. The Prince yelled in shock and splayed out his arms and legs in a vain effort to stabilize himself, but all that happened was he tripped Breca as she stumbled around saying, "The Cheshire Cat! I just saw the Cheshire Cat!"

She went over the side fairly gracefully, fought her way back up to the surface, and said, "The water's warm!"

"Yes, it is, isn't," agreed the Prince. "It's known as the Giant's Stream."

"What? More like a river." She paused a moment, bobbing gently in the slight current. "Oh, get me out of here, would you?"

He grabbed her by the collar, as politely as possible, and tried to haul her over the side. Unfortunately, a man who has difficulty rowing a small boat will inevitably have difficulty pulling a hundred and ten pound dead weight over the side of said small boat. Breca, however, had no trouble pulling him into the river with her.

They floated and watched the boat go on its way alone.

"Looks quite lonely, doesn't it."

"It does," agreed the Prince, trying to doggy-paddle.

She raised her arms and flopped both hands down in the water in an oh-well gesture, splashing Stoat. "Now that we're both here, explain to me about why this is called the Giant's Stream."

"Oh, don't worry about it. It comes from a stationary rain cloud about two miles upstream. Rain cloud actually ran for office recently," he added conversationally. "I sort of like the way it thinks, but, you know what they say, you can never choose your political allies—"

"But why the Giant's—"

"Well. Dalyas the Giant discovered it, see. The stream, I mean."

"Oh. That's all right, then."

"Yes. The giants have been using it as a shower ever since, I believe."

Breca looked with sudden distrust and apprehension at a piece of what appeared to be seaweed that floated by near her.

"Really," she said.

"Uh-huh. Um. Maybe this might be a good time to mention that I can't swim?"

"Oh! Sorry. Strike out for the bank, I suppose—" Breca did not have a lot of experience with swimming, either, or drowning, for that matter. All she knew was that swimming was good, drowning bad, and if you didn't swim you were going to drown very fast. Stoat was quite buoyant, but even he couldn't float forever.

"I don't know," said Stoat, "it's quite a bit away—" But he started making stiff, feeble motions with his arms, less like a doggie-paddle and more like a cow-paddle. Breca struck out herself and tried not to laugh.

"Oh, no. Rather don't think I'm going to make it," said Stoat hopelessly after a few minutes in which he made no headway at all.

"Oh, come on—"

"No. No, I'm going down, Alice." He turned towards her and swallowed hard, inadvertently chugging a few mouthfuls of river water in his effort to be dramatic. "Listen. I just wanted to tell you—"

"What?" Breca asked, drawn into his golden-eyed gaze despite herself.

"I think I'm in love with you."

Breca laughed, and pushed him.

"Oh, knock it off, Stoat. Oh, sorry," she added as the Prince's head went under water.

He didn't come back up.

"Stoat?"

Bubbles.

"Stoat?"

More bubbles.

"Stoat!"

His head broke the water as he gasped in oxygen. The first thing he said was, "I do believe you saved my life!"

"I didn't, I didn't even touch you!" She wrapped her arms around him and tried to hold him up.

"No, I think you did," said Stoat with definitiveness. He looked up at her with adoration. "Thank you, Alice."

"Shut up, don't talk," suggested Breca, kicking.

Abruptly, they didn't seem to be drifting so much, and the Prince seemed to grow a couple of inches.

"I say!" he said. "I can reach here!"

"Anyway, what were you going to say?"

"Hmm?"

"Before all that happened with the boat."

The Prince put his arms behind his head and thought seriously. "Oh, yes, I remember," he said finally. Breca waited, patiently. He looked over at her and smiled. "I'll tell you later."

She shrugged, feeling under her shoulders the roughness of the treebark she leaned against. Though they were in the middle of a forest, it wasn't actually a tree, but simply a foot-thick piece of bark sticking up out of the ground. Very convenient. She was rather leery of trees now.

Speaking of which—

"Stoat," she started slowly, "did you see anything unusual in the trees before the boat went over?"

"Mmm— don't think so, no. Why?"

"Well, I think I did." She looked up at the lacy branches far above her head, and lifted her brows. Bark and branches, but no actual intervening tree— now that was odd. "I thought I saw— a puddy tat."

Stoat blinked. "I beg your pardon?"

"Never mind. It's not important. I saw the Cheshire Cat. At least, I think I did. At least, it smiled at me. I think it was a cat, and normal cats don't grin, do they? Or— do they, Stoat?"

"They might,' said Stoat thoughtfully, "if they were very happy. Alice, I know I've only known you since just after lunch, but would you marry me?"

"Oh. That's what you were going to say?"

"Yes, that's right."

"But you said you'd tell me later."

"It is later. What do you think?"

"Well—" she said, pausing a moment to make it seem more dramatic an answer than it actually was. "It's certainly something to consider."

"*It is?*"

She smiled at his hopeful, eager face. "Yes. Of course it is."

It wasn't the Prince who asked if it was, of course, but Axford, who, in the spirit of insatiable curiosity, had been spying on them all afternoon, and now sat behind a nearby clump of bushes. He clapped a hand over his mouth as soon as the words slipped out, and heaved a sigh of relief that, apparently, Breca thought Stoat had said it, and Stoat hadn't noticed anything amiss. Although, to be perfectly frank, Stoat probably wouldn't notice anything amiss if the situation involved twelve baboons balancing on the head of a pin while an eagle delivered a hippo's baby in the background. You can be nice and say this was because Stoat was so in love with Alice that he found it impossible to think about anything but her, but really it was because Stoat just wasn't very bright.

Breca knew it was Axford, though.

She also knew of an age-old equation: Prince plus girl equals King and Queen. The knowledge made her smile secretly if rather nastily to herself. She was not particularly fond of the present Queen.

Prince Stoat plus Breca/Alice equals King and Queen of Wonderland.

High above her head on an unanchored limb, the Cheshire Cat grinned, too, but this was not so much because it was naturally cheerful, as much as its teeth were rather large. As a matter of fact it should have had braces to try and correct the problem quite a long time ago, but it couldn't afford the extensive dental procedures it would require.

There was a moment of pure silence over the countryside, in which someone arrived, having been called by fate and his own desires, without a suitcase but carrying several thousands of years of emotional baggage.

Isn't life, he was thinking, *grand.*

The Queen, too, knew about the age-old equation, and so she was considering taking some rather drastic actions (exacerbated somewhat by the cheering crowds outside her palace who were chanting their heroine's name over and over) when Widden showed up.

He looked a little shaky— he'd only been out of the stocks for a few hours, and only spent part of that time conscious after being hit with a flying hairbrush. Most of that consciousness had been spent in a beleaguered pet shop down the road that, against all expectations, seemed to only sell badgers and hedgehogs.

"Milady," he said. "A—gentleman to see you."

The Queen put down the stick she'd been beating the dog with and ascended to the throne. She took a few minutes to smooth her hair, adopt the proper regal attitude, and kick the dog one final time.

"Show him in," she said, with a grand, expansive, and ultimately pointless gesture.

Widden bowed obsequiously and went out. After a moment, the door opened, but no-one came through it. It closed, opened, closed. It did this a few more times without anyone showing, like a mouth that's not quite sure what it wants to say. Finally, with the air of having learnt the value of building anticipation, someone walked in.

He looked to be a bit over seven feet tall, and swathed in a dark robe. A cowl concealed his face. If he had turned around, she would have seen a sickle in the clever and newly-patented holster strapped to his belt. Something about his form mesmerized her, made her sit up and pay more attention. The Queen had never been much for paying attention to things, but she was oddly compelled at this point to do so.

He advanced to the throne and slowly lifted his head.

There was nothing there.

Just darkness.

She could see right to the back of the cowl.

Then, slowly at first, then faster, a face began to appear, and a body with it. The features were sketched in slowly, then filled, took on a dark texture like a photo negative, then began lightening until a man with grey eyes, greyish skin, grey hair, and suddenly baggy robes stood in front of her. His face was quite handsome, but very much on the disturbing side in its quiet seriousness.

The Queen cleared her throat. "A nice trick, if you can manage it," she said. "I've been thinking of learning it myself."

He didn't speak, but in his eyes something flared for a moment.

The Queen caught her breath. "Ah, yes," she said. "I've been waiting for you."

Breca, mindful of her duties to her role, went and visited, accompanied by a devoted Stoat. She visited the people who lived on the right side of the town's main street—

—then she visited the people who lived on the left side of the town's main street—

—and then, thoroughly exhausted, somewhat ill, and definitely a bit disturbed, she ditched Stoat as politely as possible and went and visited the pub. This was where most of the people were, anyway.

Everyone stared at her as she came in, but it'd been a long day so she was quite used to it by now and, despite being British and so having a predisposition towards such behavior, was neither offended or nervous.

She stumbled over to the bar, noticed the woman there was staring at her open-mouthed, and pulled herself together long enough for thirty seconds of Winsome Alice, which she'd been doing at people all day. She thoroughly detested it and the rather mean-minded, in-the-spirit-of-curiosity cruelty that passed for her sense of humor was beginning to assert itself.

She placed herself neatly on the stool, settled her dress, looked up, and said in a gruff, Scottish bass, "Ach, get me a lager, will ye, hon? Had a tirin' dae."

Soul Train jumped and backed off.

"Interesting," said Axford, who had been following her all afternoon and only narrowly avoided doing more talking when he wasn't meant to. She'd known he was around somewhere, anyway, so his self-control had been for nothing. He took the seat next to her as Soul Train shoved Breca's drink across the bar top without so much as a stray word about payment passing her lips, and then hurried away. "And highly effective, I see."

"Yes, it is, isn't it," agreed Breca. "I call it Businessman in Drag. Of course it works better here. Really they see that sort of thing all the time at home."

"You'll give yourself away."

"No, I'd never. Sell, yes, for good money, but never give freely. Mind you," she added, thinking of certain things that had happened during the day, "some people seem disposed to take without asking first."

"Oh yes?"

"But I gave them a good slap."

"Oh, good."

She peered sharply at him but he was drinking her lager.

"Axford, do you mean to tell me you don't care what happens to me?"

"Of course I care! What're you talking about? You're putting Wonderland back on track, aren't you? Everything's going great."

She stared into the drink. It bubbled like chemicals in a laboratory and she wasn't entirely taken with the smell either.

"I wonder—" she said.

"Well, this is the place for it."

She drank it anyway.

"And what about Stoat?"

"What about the stoat?" asked Axford, innocently.

"Don't give me that. I know it was you behind that tree."

"Tree?"

"Knock it off, Axford."

"Knock what off, Breca?"

"Oh, I don't know," said Breca tiredly. "Whatever you like."

Axford paused a moment, then pushed the half-empty mug onto the floor. It shattered into several pieces, which stared at each other in distrust and began crawling underneath the bar.

"Ah, yes," he said, looking up, "everything's much clearer now."

Breca looked in his familiar face, and smiled. "We met in a pub. Remember?"

"Yes. Almost a whole week ago, it was."

"Yeah. A week tomorrow, isn't it? D'you think we should celebrate our anniversary? I mean, a whole week spent together when neither of us are particularly likeable anyway, and all sorts of weird stuff was going on on top of that, and even though we argued a lot, yet we still didn't kill each other."

"Yeah. Amazing."

Breca leaned her head on her hand. "I really like you, Axford. Even better than Death. Even better than Stoat, who is nice like pie."

"I'm glad." Axford considered the ramifications of being nice like pie. Would you not get eaten? Or eaten ever more than usual? He shook his head.

"Why?" inquired Breca.

"Because if it wasn't for you liking me, I'd probably be back down in the Queen's dungeon, rotting away."

"Why should you be? You're a hero, Axford! You can do anything you want!"

There was a brief, rather intense moment when their eyes met and Axford's mouth fumbled for something to say.

"You know what, you're right," he said, jumped off his chair, and ran out the door.

Breca, sitting now by herself, pressed her knuckles to her forehead and said, "I knew I should have kept my mouth shut."

"Problem, Miss Alice?" said Soul Train, braving her heroine's oddities.

"Yes, now I'll have to marry Stoat," complained Breca. "Why doesn't anything work properly in real life? It's all so neatly set up in books."

Soul Train did her best to look sympathetic while not having the faintest idea what Alice was saying. She struggled for something encouraging, insightful, or at least coherent to say.

"Same again?" is what she ended up with.

"Why not?" said Breca, and heaved a sigh. "I'll need a new glass, though. The last one got upset, depressed, and suicidal in rapid succession, and did a runner off the bar top."

"I don't have any more glasses," said Soul Train, reckoning at this point that having an expression on her face at all would probably not help.

"Well, just give me a bottle then."

"It doesn't come in *bottles*. Comes in barrels—"

"Oh, all trouble comes in *Barrels*," groaned Breca.

"— like any normal liquor would."

Breca was going to make an extraordinarily brilliant comment about normalcy in this setting, but as she sucked in breath to launch it forth she took another look at the face of the woman on the other side of the bar and realized it would be wasted. Besides which, after dealing with all sizes and shapes of beings all day, she found she just didn't have the strength.

"Well, then," she said. "Two kegs of your best, then."

Some people, despite all evidence to the contrary, still believe that everything happens for a reason, though in fact things happen and then people make up the reasons later. Life has a lot in common with crossword puzzles if you look at it the right way.

Maybe it was better like this.

At any rate the alcohol had comfortably padded her senses when Comfit ran in, limping slightly, and told her that Death was up at the castle, and making quite a hit with the Queen.

"Yes, do you mind just putting your name down in the visitor's book, please? A mere formality. It helps to keep track."

He, noting briefly and with passing interest that the name above his was Samuel Clemens, wrote slowly, laboriously, and with ridiculously small, neat handwriting.

"Death is left-handed," she observed. "Interesting." She leaned between him and the book. "Freedrish Death," she read out.

"Fredreiche," said death stiffly. "It's like 'Frederick' except it makes people sit up and take notice."

"Of course, how silly of me." She flashed him a smile that said if he agreed with her on the silliness issue, he'd regret it. "May I call you Fred?"

Death stared at her warily. "Is there anything on earth that could stop you?"

She coughed violently and tried to cover up with a laugh.

"So. Why are you here? Or perhaps, rather than getting down to business at once, you would prefer me to be a bit friendlier at first ."

"No, I think you're quite friendly enough." He removed her

encroaching hand from his shoulder.

"I mean, I *can* ask questions and be caring, you know. I just don't do it normally because no-one around here is important enough to even pretend to care about. But, in this case— I mean, you *are* a visiting dignitary. A handsome visiting dignitary. A handsome, *dramatic* visiting dignitary. You look quite sharp in black. And you're from Alice's world, no less. And you *are* the reigning power there." Death said nothing. "Aren't you? Aren't you, Fred?"

"Not in so many words,' he answered finally and with care. "I mean yes, the buck does eventually end up stopping with me, but it's not like *I* get to make the decisions. It sort of just happens. Once humanity starts living, they don't seem to stop, till they hit a brick wall, so to speak. Some of them literally. And who knows how long I'll last, anyway? Suppose nobody were to die any more."

"What a *terr*ible thought," purred the Queen.

"I know! I mean, there's me out of a job. Not to mention the undertakers. You know, I never realized it till just now, but I really like undertakers. There's something honest about them. It's kind of like we're— oh, I don't know. Brothers under the skin, like. Um, metaphorically speaking."

"Right. And so do you enjoy your work?" It was not common for the Queen to be polite, but she found she was watching his mouth move rather attentively.

"Er—" said Death. He'd not come across this question before. "Well, I find it quite— interesting. I mean, you certainly get around, meet lots of people and such. Celebrities are interesting because they try to buy me off. *Do you want my autograph*, they say, and get terribly upset when I say *Fine* and then after they put a scribble in my book I end up taking their lives as well. They tend to scream *I thought we had a deal!*" He sniffed. "Drama queens. Some try to cheat me, too. They say *Do you want to play chess for my life* and I say *No thanks, I don't know the rules and I'd rather stick to Monopoly if you don't mind*, and they say *Monopoly! But it takes so long!* And anyway if I ever do play, they say I cheat. I don't like to be accused of cheating. I am honest, basically. More than *they* are at any rate. Some of them hide when they think I'm coming— under the bed, in closets, anywhere. Had one fellow lock himself in a completely sealed inner chamber, no windows, no air ducts, no nothing. It wasn't actually his time to die, not for another few years, but he suffocated, you see." Death trailed off, grinning thoughtfully to himself. It wasn't a smile of amusement, but Death had, after all, had plenty of time to work up a sense of irony as well as humor.

"Fascinating," said the Queen, but her eyes looked a little glazed. "And now, won't you please tell me why you're here."

Death cleared his throat, folded his hands and looked serious. "I'm here because— I'm in love."

The Queen stood still. "Death is in love," she murmured. "I rather think that was the plot of a novel I read recently."

"It makes no difference whether it's an original idea or not," said Death sharply. "The fact is, it's the way things are. You can't choose who you love. It's certainly not like I chose Breca—

The Queen's head shot up. Her eyes pierced Death's borrowed face. Or would have done, if he'd been looking at her, but he was staring moodily into the middle distance.

"Breca," she said, then screeched it. "*BRECA!*"

"Yes, Breca," said Death, somewhat offended. "You know her? Breca Sigh, Breca Marie Sigh, nineteen years old, red hair, hazel eyes, pixie face—"

"*Red* hair? Are you sure she's not blonde?"

"Ah, well, she'd be wearing a wig."

"How do you know?"

"Well, she's masquerading as Alice, isn't she? Word on the street is, she's taken in everyone here pretty well. Even the ruler of Wonderland! Well, if you can call her a ruler. I heard the woman is dumb as a post and has a body like a toothbrush with arms and the ruling power of a piece of fried lavatory paper— oh," he said, noticing the crown and the throne for, apparently, the first time.

The Queen's head exploded, quietly. Death patiently helped her pick up the pieces.

"This Breca," she said, once she'd been put back together, "she is— important to you?"

"Yes. Very much."

"And does she feel the same about you?"

"She—" said Death, and hesitated. Though ostensibly he had been convinced that, once Breca found out he had a body now, all her objections would be overcome, the dream sessions they'd had recently were certainly bothersome. "Well, after all," he said finally, "it's not like she's got a lot of choice. I mean, if she *agrees* to go with me, naturally it'd be nicer—"

"I'm sure," said the Queen, grinning like a shark.

"But if she doesn't—" Death looked worried.

"Oh, I'm sure you could take her. If," said the Queen.

"What do you mean, *if?*" Death demanded. "That isn't even a complete sentence, *if.* Why don't you brush up your grammar?"

"Oh, shut up," said the Queen.

"*You* shut up!"

They glared at each other for a minute. Then the Queen's face took on a cunning look, or, at least, what passed for a cunning look. She was unused to making this expression, and it was so at odds with what she normally looked like that her features quite changed. Death tilted his head to one side in utter surprise.

"You know," she said, "while you're here, you might as well

practice your art for the good of the kingdom."

"Sorry?" said Death blankly. "My what?"

"Your art. Your— deadly art."

"Oh." Even connoisseurs hadn't been known to refer to it that way.

"You know what they say. Seven lively, eighth deadly."

Death rubbed his chin. "No, actually I've never heard anyone say that, anyone at all."

"You see, my dear Fredreiche, I have enemies," the Queen went on, ignoring him. "And— I'm in the right, of course, it's all their fault that we're enemies at all. We *could* be very good friends. Just as you and I could be very good friends."

He went and sat on the very high throne. It took him a few minutes to climb the stairs. He stared thoughtfully down at the floor, and a grin appeared on his face. "Hey," he said, "I can see your house from up here."

"I'll make you a deal," said the Queen. Death raised his eyebrows at her.

"You're offering to make a deal with Death?"

"Yes."

"Do you have any idea what a dreadful cliché that is?"

"I don't care."

"No,' he said thoughtfully, "I suppose you don't." He shook his head in silence for a minute. "What are the terms?"

"I give you free reign, Breca and all," she said, "if you also take care of a few people I don't much like."

"I didn't come to take any of your people," said Death. "I came to get mine, is all."

"But this is *my* land, you see, Fredreiche. I run it. If you want to take someone out of it without their permission, you have to have mine. As I understand it," she went on, "you're mortal at the moment, correct? That, may I say, *stunning* body of yours doesn't possess any powers beyond your most basic function, and of course, when I say 'most basic' I'm referring to the least fun one. So what are you going to do about it?"

He stared at her for a bit, his mind racing. "You have a devious mind," he said finally. "Congratulations."

"Yes, I know. Thank you."

"So who do you want me to ice?"

"What?"

"Bump off."

"Excuse me?"

"Who is it," said Death, patiently, "that you want me to take with me when I go?"

"Oh, mostly it's just these two girls— they shouldn't be a problem. They're not particularly large or strong or anything." She laughed sharply. "As a matter of fact they have no power whatsoever."

"Really." Death studied her, his hands on his hidden hips. "Well, why do you want them gone then?"

The Queen's eye twitched. "It's a— political thing. Complicated."

"I'm sure I could manage to understand it, if you use very short words."

He waited.

The Queen thought frantically. "Well," she said, "er, they've been plotting against me from the start, you see? They want the throne for themselves. They'll do anything to get it. Including trying to get rid of me."

"But they can't, right? No death in Wonderland, till just recently."

"Which is another part of the deal," she hurried on. "You take Breca, you take the Twins, and you *on no account* take me. Got it?"

Death narrowed his eyes at her. "Is there something you're not telling me?"

"Of course. Not."

"There was a little bit of a pause in there just now, between *of course* and *not*. That's somewhat worrying, I must admit."

"I just speak like that naturally," she assured him. "A conversational hiatus, a penny on the tracks of my train of thought. Shake on it?"

"Actually, when it comes right down to it, I'd prefer you didn't touch me." He rubbed his hands together, "So, when can I get Breca? Where is she?"

"Oh, no you don't!" she said, getting in between him and the door as he turned towards them. "First the Twins. Then your girlfriend."

"Why?"

"Because."

"You don't trust me?"

"Only about as far as I could comfortably throw you," said the Queen sweetly.

Death gave her a measuring-up sort of glance that seemed to suggest he was thinking wistfully of how far he could throw her, if he got a good running start. "Fine," he said. "Twins first. Where are they?"

"Oh, we keep them in the basement. But listen, Fred, we've got time for dinner first. I mean, no hurries, right?"

"No hurries, mate," said Death, scowling. "It's just that I borrowed this body from a guy, and I promised I'd have it back by Thursday, so I'd like to get this thing over with as soon as possible. And where is Breca, anyway?"

"It doesn't matter," said the Queen, smiling with a certain brittleness. "I'm sending out guards to collect her, and that will be that."

"Where will you put her?"

"I'll keep her safe. As a matter of fact," she mused, "I know exactly how to do it—"

"Do I have time for a drink before dinner?" Death asked plaintively.

It was getting dark. Breca stepped lightly along the street, tripping slightly over her shoes. Three barrels of something unidentifiable but undeniably alcoholic had sent her into a sort of gentle whirl.

She hummed to herself. If a human from her world had been there, and been able to cut through the off-key, stilted sequence of notes, he might have been able to recognize the tune as "*Love Me Tender*".

Something slid along through the darkness behind her. There was a momentary gleam as light bounced off teeth, but that was done purely for effect. It was a good effect, too, but lost on Breca as she had her eyes closed.

She heard the slight rustling sound, though, and whirled around and stared wildly into the shadows. Now that it had her attention, whatever it was did the light-shining-off-teeth trick again.

"Oh," she said, relieved. After the incident with the cat in the trees that afternoon, she'd been hoping he'd show up again. "It's you."

"No," said a silky voice, "it's not," and ran its tongue over its teeth rather dramatically.

"A green tongue?" said Breca, squinting at it hardily. "Is that a medical condition?"

"Not really. Not a recognized one anyway."

"Huh. And you're here for what, now?"

"I've been sent by the Queen take you captive. Go on, run. I'd be happy to chase."

"Oh. See, I thought you were the Cheshire Cat. So I'm a little surprised."

A low growl cut through the air. "I don't like cats."

"Why not?" said Breca innocently.

He stepped forward, into the light, and stood formidably.

"Aha, of course," she said, nodding knowingly, and pointing at him with a slightly wavering finger. "All loan sharks hate cats— a well-known fact."

"I'm *not* a loan shark."

"What then— a fourth-rate lawyer on the make?"

"No." He frowned mightily.

"A used-car salesman who lost his checked jacket?"

"A *wolf*."

"A what?"

He grinned at her, with teeth that could have brought down an elephant if the body could have kept up.

"A wolf. The Queen's Wolf."

"Ah," said Breca, nodding at him deeply. "I would have gotten it eventually."

Chapter Thirteen

Axford Barrel stumbled his way back into the pub, having tried to do whatever he wanted, and failed.

He would have explained it, to anyone who would listen, like this:

He'd brought back Alice, right, or an Alice, anyway, and made the whole country happy. He was, therefore, a hero.

But this didn't help at all when he'd tried to take that Dodo's wallet, because the Dodo had never seen Axford Barrel before, and didn't recognize him, and didn't appreciate the hero trying to steal his wallet.

This led Axford to the theory that heroism wasn't a lot of good without fame, as well.

It also led him to a large bruise on his cheekbone, and an ache in his leg and his ribs.

Heroism wasn't a lot of good, when you were still several feet shorter than the crazed long-beaked Dodo who is attacking you just because you lifted his wallet without asking permission first.

"I don't know," he said to Soul Train, who watched him with eagle eyes, "people just have no respect."

But it worried him. He seemed to have lost his touch since he'd brought Breca to Wonderland. Not only that, but a lot of his enthusiasm as well. Maybe he shouldn't have run away from Breca in the middle of their last conversation. She probably thought he was terribly rude. And there was, of course, the problem of Prince Stoat.

He sighed sharply and shifted on the stool. Soul Train leaned in expectantly.

"It's no use," he told her. "I don't have any money. And you won't give me a drink out of the goodness of your heart, that's for sure. As a matter of fact— do you actually possess a heart, Soul Train? I've never seen any evidence of it."

"I had it removed a year or two ago," she replied seriously. "It was getting in the way. Hearts are bad things for pub-owners to have. All that business of people wandering in and making puppy eyes at you. Gets downright expensive."

"Yeah, I know how you feel," said Axford absentmindedly. He examined the wood of the bar top and felt a person slide onto the seat next to him. The person seemed to be having some trouble. Axford glanced up marginally and saw that it was on account of the man's robe being caught over the stool.

The fellow straightened it out, and said, "Give me your biggest glass of your strongest whatever, please. Alright?" and adjusted his sickle.

"Say, I know you, you're Death," said Axford, not altogether pleased.

"Yes," said Death, not altogether pleased either at being recognized, and glancing around to see if anyone else had noticed. "I, er, expect the robe was a bit of a giveaway."

"Yeah," said Axford, "and the cowl. And the sickle. And, er, the horse—"

Death glanced over his shoulder. "Oh. Ha ha. Yeah. He follows me everywhere. Hopelessly devoted, I guess."

"Really."

"Won't let me ride him, though."

"Oh."

"Uh-huh. You look a little familiar. Cheers," Death added, as Soul Train thumped a mug down in front of him. He took a long drink, throwing his head back. Axford watched his Adam's apple moving up and down.

The cowl started to slip, and Death grabbed at it and pushed it forward again.

"A little familiar," he repeated, setting his now half-empty tarn down in front of him and returning his gaze to Axford.

"I don't know why," said Axford. "I've lived my whole life in Wonderland, till recently that is."

Death licked his lips thoughtfully. Then his eyes darkened and he said, "Oh."

"What? Stomach ache? It gets you like that sometimes. You should try the soup."

"No. I just realized where I've seen you."

"Where?"

"You're the bugger who took Breca away," Death growled.

"What?" cried Axford, increasingly agitated. "How do *you* know?"

"I saw you outside the pub that night."

"Oh," he said, and, alarmed by the expression on Death's face, started to explain. "I wouldn't have taken her, except I *needed* her." Judging by the outraged jealousy he saw in Death's eyes, this was not the best way of putting things. "I mean, *Wonderland* needed her." He leaned closer to Death, casting glances around to ensure that none of the other denizens of the pub were paying attention to this. "I was sent to look for Alice, okay? And Breca said she'd been dead for years probably. So I had to find a substitute, didn't I?"

"Why did you need Alice?"

"Well, you know— since she left that last time, Wonderland's really gone to seed."

"Huh." Death reached back in his capacious memory with a visible effort. Then he smiled. "Oh, yes, I read that book. It was quite good. I enjoyed it."

"Book?" said Axford, blankly.

Death gave him a sideways glance. "So out of all the girls in all the pubs in all the world, you take my Breca."

"Yeah, basically. Uh-huh." Axford gave him a weak grin. "Buy me a drink?"

"I really ought to pound you flat." Death examined his hands. They had long, thin fingers that could easily have met around Axford's neck. "It's just that I've only had this body for a few days now, and I'm not sure how it would stand up to the strain."

Axford raised his eyebrows politely.

"Best not to risk it, then."

"See," Death went on, "the man who had it before me didn't exactly take care of it. Anytime he put on a few pounds, he went on a starvation diet instead of going to the gym. I mean, the muscles are all— feel that," he directed, holding an arm up in front of Axford's face. Axford squeezed it obligingly and made fairly meaningless noises that could have been derogatory or appreciative. "Feel that? Like cooked spaghetti. I mean— maybe *I* ought to take it to the gym. Do you have gyms here? Beef it up a little, what do you think?"

"Well," said Axford, and cleared his throat. "You'd have to buy gym clothes, for a start. Ahem. Do those robes come in Spandex?"

Death glared at him, then whapped him on the back of his head with the flat of his hand.

"Try not to be such a twit, man. Get with the times."

"I'll— I'll try, sir."

"Spandex is *out*, little man."

"Right." Privately, Axford thought to himself, he could be forgiven. Who could have guessed Death would be so petty? He rubbed the back of his head, carefully.

"At any rate, it's a nice place you've got here, gyms or not. Nice country. Mind you, the Queen is a bit of hard to take."

"Yes, she certainly is," Axford heartily concurred.

Death whapped him again. "Are you saying traitorous and

dastardly things against your Queen, little man?"

"No!" said Axford. "No! I was just agreeing with you! You're a visitor to this country, the polite thing to do is agree with any statement you make, no matter how idiotic it is!"

"Well, that's alright then," said Death, somewhat appeased. He narrowed his eyes at Axford to make sure he didn't say anything else traitorous.

"The brandy pretty good here, is it?"

"I wouldn't know," said Axford. "I can't afford anything really alcoholic, so I mostly only order soup."

"Uh-huh. Well. Can't do soup. Don't like it. Too hot. Got any good stuff?" he called to Soul Train.

"What are you asking her for?" hissed Axford. "Of course she's going to say they've got good stuff, she owns the place."

"Well, actually," called Soul Train back, "most of it is pretty rotten."

Death threw his hands in the air. "Honesty! Common honesty, in a place like this! And they said it'd never happen!" He laughed.

"In that case," said Axford, with the spare beginnings of a grin, "buy me a drink?"

Breca sat in the darkness of the dungeons and tried not to breathe deeply. There had, apparently, been many others occupying this cell before, and they'd left behind reminders, most in olfactory form.

She tried to remember everything Axford had told her about the current political situation here, looking for a clue to why she might be locked up. Of course, if the Queen knew about the Movement to Make Alice Queen (MMAQ, the more public version of the rapidly-escalating but still very secret Breca Becoming Queen initiative, or the BBQ, although very few people knew about this organization and it seemed to have been named just for the resultant acronym) that a few Wonderland residents had dreamed up, maybe that had something to do with it.

She did remember that Axford said the Queen was very experienced at effective jealousy. This wasn't, at the moment, particularly reassuring, because he'd also, when recounting his own adventures, mentioned torture.

Of course, many of the things Axford said were better taken with a grain of salt— or, in some cases, the entire shaker. She found rather difficult to believe the statement that he had undergone having his leg slowly gnawed off by mad weasels and not so much as flinched.

"Why've you still got two legs then?" she had wanted to know, and he said, "What makes you think I started out with two?"

So then she asked him to show her where the third one had been. This had been a mistake.

At any rate—

She leaned into the bars of the cell and tapped Wolf on the shoulder. He spun round and growled at her. "Well, goodness, I only tapped you!"

"I don't like being tapped." He had dropped into a kind of alert crouch, but she could see his knees wobble from the strain.

"All the same," she said, rolling her eyes at him dramatically, "it's not like I pulled your tail or something. I was just wondering whether this being locked up thing involved torture of any kind."

"Why do you want to know?"

"I need something to look forward to." She banged on the bars with the flat of her hand. "I mean, come on. Anything is better than being locked up with only you for company."

Wolf grinned and leaned close. His stomach rumbled, on cue. "Anything?"

"Well—" She moved back. "Almost anything."

The grin stayed put. "In that case, dearest *Alice*, you should be grateful that there are bars between us."

"But— you have the keys," she pointed out.

"Exactly."

He turned around to face front again. She sighed and moved back to the stone slab that was, supposedly, a cot. She lay on it and rearranged the striped clothes they'd given her. They were quite a bit too big, and, oddly enough, particolored.

"This thing's not very comfortable," she said, in reference to the slab. "Why don't you lot invest in mattresses? I mean, this is the *royal* dungeon. The Queen could probably threaten the mattress-maker and get them for free."

"I'll make a note," said the Wolf. He sounded exasperated, probably because he was. Breca did that to people. Sooner or later, she'd get to you.

Death was having a rather good time. Axford Barrel, while not exactly stimulating companionship, was a very good listener.

Actually, Death had to admit, he was quite a bit more interesting after the first half hour spent in the pub, drinking steadily.

"Honestly, you would not believe," said Death. "I mean honestly, I would not, I mean, you would not believe, honestly. You wouldn't."

"I believe you," said Axford, solidly agreeable as all good drinking buddies are.

Death blinked. "No, you're not supposed to."

"Oh. Then I don't."

"But I haven't told you yet."

"Don't," suggested Axford. "Just let me relish it for a moment."

Death let him relish it for a moment. "But if I don't tell you, you won't be able to not believe me."

"I don't care."

"You don't care." Death sneezed. "Ah, that's the problem. People just don't care. Whoa, that was a good sneeze just now. Didja, Axford, didja, didja ever? Didja ever investigate the properties of a *really* good sneeze?"

"I don't sneeze," said Axford.

Death widened his eyes to alarming proportions. "You don't *sneeze*? Axford, you don't *sneeze*? Why don't you sneeze, Axford?"

"I don't know. I just— don't."

"Wow. You are missing out. Some life you must lead."

"Well, *I* like it."

"Yeah, sure. What's the alternative?"

They stared at each other. Something sharp and emotional clicked in the air. They knew their places in the world, and out of it.

"Right," said Death. "Listen, call me Fred, won't you?"

"And you can call me Axford."

"I already do. Axford."

"In that case, call me Mr. Barrel."

"Yes, Mr. Barrel!" Death saluted.

"I'm thinking Mr. Barrel is a good name to start my new career off with."

"Oh, yeah?"

"What do you think?"

Death gulped the last of his drink down, belched, and said, "Smooooooooth."

"You like it?"

"I *like* it. What career are you thinking of?"

"I don't know. I'm open to options."

"Yeah. Well, you can't beat that, being open to options. Become an undertaker. Then we could work together."

"Yeah?"

"Yeah. Actually, I'm trying to find a good career move for me, actually. I'm thinking, maybe, stripy robes, actually. Just for a change, actually."

"Huh," said Axford, carefully leaning his chin on his hand. He had tried this a few times now and missed, hence his caution. "Well, like, you're Death, and you work in the dying business, so, when you think about it, being you *is* a good career move."

"I never thought about it like that," said Death.

"Well, you should. Makes sense, doesn't it?"

"It's certainly a point," Death admitted. He plucked at the front of his robe, and squinted down at it. "On the other hand, stripes are very fashionable."

"Agreed." Axford saluted with his tankard.

They both had another drink each.

"So," said Axford slowly, "like, what's your ideal job, then? You must have seen some doozies in your time, eh?"

"In my time," said Death, "which is forever, by the way, yes, I have seen some what you might call doozies. The cruelty of the human race is *amazing*. Think about it. Even the things they do to themselves. I mean, every bungee jumper must have at least one mortal enemy, right? How hard is it for mortal enemies to find bolt cutters, or axes, or something else with a sufficiently sharp edge? Just imagine this, Axford, just imagine this— a man— on a pogo-stick— in a minefield."

Axford nodded. "Amazing."

"I know. I know. It's enough to make you cry." Death wiped his eyes. "And then there's the deathbeds."

"Yeah."

Death, still misty eyed and looking into the middle space, said heavily, "I always feel kind of honored whenever anyone mentions deathbeds."

They were quiet for a minute, then Death said, "Look, it's been nice talking with you, Axford— I, er, hope we never have to meet again."

"Me, too," said Axford sincerely.

They shook hands.

"That's a nice time-piece, there," said Axford, referring to the one on death's left wrist.

"Oh, thanks. It came with the body when I borrowed it. Actually, it's the only thing I kept, apart from the underwear."

Axford twisted his head to look at it. "Is *that* the time?"

"No. Time is just a concept people use to ensure that they're late for dentist appointments," Death explained. "This is a wristwatch." He let his sleeve slip back over it.

"Very nice."

"And now I have to go. I'm, uh, having dinner with the Queen."

"Good luck," said Axford.

"Don't need it," said Death. "But thanks anyway."

"Oh, and avoid the spaghetti sauce. There's a reason it's that greenish color."

"Why is— oh, never mind. Don't want to know. Thanks," said Death again, and flashed him a slightly drunken, sweet smile as he went out the door.

Left to himself, Axford examined the watch with interest. He considered that it was a good sign that even Death didn't notice when his watch went missing. Maybe Axford hadn't lost his touch after all.

He was still grinning to himself when the raven flapped in,

panting. It landed on the bar in front of him.

"Oh, hullo," said Axford pleasantly. "Where've you been?"

"Spying," gasped the raven.

"Find out anything interesting?"

"Yes— the Queen's got a crush on Death—"

"Don't tell me you're jealous."

"And she had Breca locked up in the cells."

"What?" Axford stared wildly at him, then thumped an irate fist on the counter top. "That treacherous, stupid, toothbrush-bodied *miscreant*— how dare she lock up Alice? After I brought her here to save Wonderland! After all that work I put in, all the effort expended, she puts Alice, the Hope of Wonderland, in the dungeons? How *dare* she!"

"Except that it's not Alice, it's Breca."

"It's the *principle* of the thing! It *could* have been Alice! Right, let's go. We have to get her out."

"Wait, stop!" wailed the raven. "She's being guarded by the Wolf, and only he and the Queen have the keys to the cell!"

Axford didn't stop at all. "We'll figure something out," he shouted over his shoulder. "Let's go! *Nobody* locks up my Breca!"

The small whirlwind of activity that was Axford Barrel slammed out the door, followed by a gloomy, morose black bird.

The denizens of the pub, who, for once in their lives, had been neglecting their drinks and instead been paying keen attention to everything that had happened in the past forty minutes, because it was none of their business and that was their favorite sort of thing, looked at each other in bewilderment.

Finally, Soul Train spoke.

"*Breca?*" she said.

Chapter Fourteen

Sneaking is notoriously difficult in a castle with talking walls, but luck seemed to be on Axford's side— or perhaps the walls were. At any rate, there was no sound in the long hallway except for the *click click click* of the raven's talons.

Axford gestured wildly at it to stop making noise. The raven watched his peculiar dancing for a moment, then said, "What?"

"Stop clicking!" Axford hissed, clenching his hands in front of him.

"Well, I can't help it," said the raven aloud, with a certain amount of sullenness. "It's too close in here to fly, and I can't walk as silently as you can. What do you expect me to do, take a run-up and slide down the hall on my feathers?"

Axford heaved a sigh. "Look," he whispered, "hop up on my shoulder, I'll carry you."

The raven cocked its head and gave Axford a sideways glance. "You sure?"

"Positive! Now come on!" Axford put a hand down so the bird could run up his arm to his shoulder— which it did, eventually, muttering to itself.

"Hey, man," it said brightly once it had gotten there, "this is really cool, you know? You normally don't let me ride on you."

"Yeah, so you owe me one," said Axford, too irritated to worry about whispering now. "So shut up!"

"Take it easy, Axford," said the raven, rather offended. It laughed suddenly. "You know what? Take a chill pill." Another birdy giggle. "That's what they say in Alice's world. It's amazing what people will talk about you in front of you if they think you're just a dumb bird. I heard this one guy talking about turnips like it wasn't a big deal at all!"

"Yes, very interesting."

"I mean, honestly, it was just turnip this, turnip that, turnips in a basket with turnip sauce, my, the turnips are doing well this year. The guy was like a health-food nut or something."

"Yeah."

"Wore funny clothes, too."

"Yeah. Hey, could you focus for a minute here?"

"But—"

"Is that *really* too much to ask?"

"That depends." The raven subsided into thought. "At any rate, I was only trying to thank you."

"Okay. I accept that."

"Okay. So, what's the plan?"

"We're going to drug the Queen, sneak into her room, steal the key, and free Breca."

"Wait a minute!" squawked the bird. "Wait just a minute, Axford Barrel! Several points come immediately to mind when listening to this so-called plan of yours. Point one: what are we expected to drug Her Majesty with?"

"This." Axford held up a small vial, half full of liquid that sloshed quietly to itself as he walked.

"Ooh, what's that?"

"The very same potion Soul Train put in our soup to get us captured, forever ago."

"Yeah, it's been a little over a week," the raven snorted. "How did you get it?"

"Well, keeping in mind that I'm a professional thief," said Axford, "what method presents itself?"

"Er— you stole it?"

"Yes. I stole it."

"Right. Fine. And, point two, how do you suggest we get the Queen to drink it?"

"We put it into her wine. You'll probably have to do that."

"Why me?" said the raven, abruptly switching to a whine. "Why should *I* have to do it? Why not you?"

"Because, although Her Majesty isn't the brightest star in the sky, presumably she would notice if a little man that she hates emptied a mysterious bottle into her drink and then proposed a toast."

"So how exactly, then, do we get her to not notice a big black bird that she doesn't appreciate as much as she should swooping down and emptying said mysterious bottle into her drink?"

"We'll burn that bridge when we come to it, raven."

"I don't like that saying, Axford."

They had gone a few more steps before the bird said, quite emotionally, "D'you know, that's the first time you've referred to me directly, personally?"

"What are you talking about? I've called you Maverick before, haven't I, and that's your name, isn't it?"

"That's the name someone *gave* me," said the bird bitterly, shifting its weight on Axford's shoulder from claw to claw. "My *true* name, for my *true* self, is raven."

"Really."

"Yes. Well. Nobody ever accused birds of having too much imagination. Not accurately, anyhow." It began to sniff emotionally, which is rather difficult to do with nothing but a beak.

"Now, look—"

"I know! I know! Look, point three, how are we supposed to steal the key from the Queen without her waking up? She keeps it around her neck!"

"That," said Axford patiently, "is what the potion is for."

The raven was silent for a minute. "Point four," it said suddenly, "Breca is guarded by the Queen's Wolf. How do you suggest we get past him and free her?"

It was Axford's turn to be quiet. Finally he said, in a monotone, "I was hoping you wouldn't ask me that, actually."

It was too late, at any rate. They had reached the door to the Queen's banquet hall, which was ajar. Axford peered cautiously through, and the raven hopped onto his head in order to see more clearly.

The Queen was seated at the head of the long, long table. Though every other place was set, no-one else had been invited, except Fred Death, who sat to her right and tried to look impassive in the light of a hundred dancing candles. He looked, mostly, nervous. This was most likely on account of the Queen, who had taken careful yet deliberate possession of his right hand and was kneading it with her knuckles.

"I was trained as a masseuse," she was saying in an interesting version of a seductive growl. "I'll give you a back rub later, if you ask me nicely."

"Urk," said Death, indistinctly.

"Right," whispered Axford to the raven, ducking his head back behind the door. He was not without sympathy for the beleaguered Death, and he reckoned the sooner the plan was put into action, the better for all concerned. "Here's the bottle—"

The raven took it carefully in its claw and Axford unstoppered it. The bird looked up at Axford with black eyes bright. The raven version of a cynical smile was on its beak, and it looked determined.

"Now, fly careful, stay level, don't drop any on the way in. We need all of it in there to get the full effect."

"What do you think I am, a rookie? I *have* flown before, you know. I'm quite accomplished at it. Bird, you know."

"Just dump it in her glass," said Axford, ignoring this. "You're going to have to do something to distract her, though. Um— swoop at her head, or something."

"Gladly," said the raven, grimly. "Here I go."

"Go," whispered Axford.

"I am going."

"Go faster."

"Right." The bird took wing.

"And so I look down," said the Queen, wrapping up what had been falsely advertised as a funny story, "and there's the man's arm, right where he'd left it!"

She laughed. It was an evil laugh, the real *mua-hah-hah* kind, which she'd been practicing daily in front of the mirror.

"Har har," said Death, looking bored.

The Queen stopped laughing, abruptly. "Oh, come on, Fred, you can't tell me that wasn't funny."

"Yes I can, just you watch me," disagreed Death. "It wasn't funny."

The Queen looked a bit bewildered in what she fondly imagined was a charmingly affected way. "But Fred, it involves the classic *elements* of a good story!"

"Such as?"

"Such as monkeys, violence, and, er, disarmament!"

"That wasn't funny either."

"Oh, come on, Death," the Queen snapped, losing her temper. "Where's your sense of humor?"

"Right where I left it. On the top of my bureau in my bedroom at home."

The Queen smiled suddenly and leant forward. "Do you think I'll ever get to see your home, Fred?"

"With my luck—" Death started, but was interrupted by a ball of black feathers which flew at the Queen's head with surprising fury.

There followed several confusing seconds in which the raven attacked the Queen repeatedly, and the Queen stumbled about the room with her arms flung about her head. She was making quite a bit of noise, but the raven at first did its duty with infuriated silence, although to himself he was thinking *Politician! Politician! Politician!*

And then it opened its beak and shouted it out.

"*Down with Politicians!*"

It may not have been the most awe-inspiring battle cry in Wonderland's history (which includes the famous "*I* built the Brooklyn Bridge!" thought up by Larkin the Knave but never actually used, as no-one had any idea what the Brooklyn Bridge was in Wonderland, and the infamous "Daddy Needs A New Set Of Drill Bits!" used by Euphonious Erroneous in the Battle of the Rusty Old

Water-tower That Nobody Really Wanted Anyway) but it was pretty catchy. Axford, waiting behind the door, felt a smile appear on his face.

It was only Death, watching this with an expression of polite interest, who noted the greenish liquid that the raven poured into the Queen's wine. It went in with a few little bubbles breaking on the surface, and then it was still.

The Queen, still howling, picked up the first thing that came to her hand— a fork— and flung it at the raven, who dodged easily. This having no effect, the Queen went for something more substantial— the fireplace poker— and swung at the bird as she ran, screaming, from the room.

But before she was out, she connected.

The raven hurtled through the air with a pained squawk and thudded into the rafter above Death's head.

It fell.

Axford, racing into the room in a flurry of consternation, found the raven lying in Death's dinner plate. He hurried over and climbed up on the table and crouched over it.

"Are you alright?" he cried.

The raven gave a despairing groan.

"Maverick? Raven? Are you okay?"

"There's—" said the raven, with a great deal of effort. "Something— you— should know—"

"What?" whispered Axford. "What is it?"

"About— the Queen—"

"What?" Axford leaned closer.

"The Queen's a— the Queen's a poli— the Queen's a—"

"*What?*" said Axford, his whisper now urgent and somewhat irritated.

"Never-mind," croaked the raven, "never-mind."

Its eyes closed.

Its breath stilled.

"What's it doing?" cried Axford, tears already welling up.

"It's dying," said death, who knew.

Axford poked the raven, prodded it, shook it, got no response, sniffed mightily and wiped his eyes. "But that can't happen. There is no—"

He looked up in shock into Death's face.

There was the sound of the Queen returning, stomping, complaining.

"Go," whispered Fred Death. "I'll take care of it."

Axford darted out as the Queen walked in, looking around with hunted eyes.

"Where is it," she said harshly. "What was it?"

She had come accompanied by three of the castle guards. They looked around rather nervously at the still room, and Death motioned them to go about their business.

"Your Majesty," he said, standing, "you have killed the raven."

"I *what*?" said the Queen. She hesitated for a few seconds before she built enough false courage to come towards him. She stared closely at the little feathered body that lay on the table like a poorly-considered centerpiece, then looked up at him in confusion. She'd never seen death happen before, but this didn't bother her unduly. It was what he was here for, anyway. "But what was it doing?"

"Attacking you," said Death matter-of-factly. "Nobody would blame it, really. Word on the street is, you're a politician. I would say it found that out and decided the world would be better off without you. As I said, no-one would blame it. Well, it tried." Death paused for a minute and shook his head. Then he resumed, and his voice was hard and bright and brittle. "But you triumphed, didn't you. He attacks you against all odds, the more fool him. You showed that feathery little berk who was boss in Wonderland."

The Queen didn't like his usage of past tense, but Death was already moving on. He raised his glass.

"A toast," he said. "May you rule as long as you live."

The Queen gave him a narrow-eyed glance, one of many she'd sent him in the past few hours, but she was not keen on subtlety and didn't take enough notice of his tone or the look of strange bitterness in his eyes. So she lifted her glass—

—and drank—

A poorly lighted room.

Death sat, naked apart from Fred's Union Jack boxers. He sat on a three-legged stool. It was very uncomfortable, but he didn't move. He hadn't moved for quite a while now. He was thinking.

His robe was displayed on a mannequin, complete with arms and a head for the cowl to conceal. He watched it like a knight on a vigil watches his armor, praying all night long.

His lips moved.

Is this who I am? Really? And who I want to be
Would I rather be completely human?
Or go back to formless shapeless bodiless force of nature?
What do I really want?

Actually, that one was easy. He could answer that, no problem.

He knew exactly what he wanted. She was sitting in a cell far below him, and it wouldn't be difficult for him to get her out, because he was Death, after all. If nothing else, it certainly opened a lot of doors.

He heaved a sigh, stood up. "Well. Glad that's over with."

It appeared to be every person's worst nightmare, that they would see themselves as they actually were, and it would turn out they were terrible people. Or, if not actually terrible, then irritating, or annoying, or unlikeable, or yes, they *were* as fat as they looked in that picture. Death had a bit of trouble with the concept of self-examination, though he would have advised anyone to do it as a cancer-prevention method. It didn't seem that bad of a nightmare, anyway. That one about the giant octopus seemed far worse— or was that just from a movie? It seemed to him that this dreaming lark was something that should be experienced at least once by everyone, but Death wasn't quite sure how to go about since every time he tried to fall asleep he ended up talking to Breca.

At any rate, the human body Death inhabited had seemed keen on introspection, so Death had given in, and he was perfectly at ease with the results.

Which was good.

Because he could have stopped it all—

But he liked Axford. Axford could have his hour. Death would grant it to him freely. And then when it was over, Breca would come to him. *It was like that song*, he thought, absently scratching his shoulder, *something about dancing with whoever you like, just remember who's taking you home.* And Breca was so homesick, he knew.

Well, okay, so it wasn't *exactly* like that song. Close enough.

Death picked up the fireplace poker and hefted it experimentally. Yes, Axford should be able to handle it.

He smiled to himself, not exactly because anything was funny (though he'd heard the phrase *It's a funny old world, innit?* and agreed with it whole-heartedly, sort of like *Boggles the mind, dunnit?* but seemed to apply more generally) but simply because everything seemed to be working out so well. He hummed quietly to himself as he put his robe back on.

He had quite good pitch, actually.

Breca, trying not to dream and failing, sighed and asked Death, "How did you know I was here, anyway?"

"Well, I *am* Death. Give me some credit."

She opened her eyes, sat up, and said loudly, "I can not get to sleep like this, Mister Wolf. It's just too *hard*."

"Telling me will make it all better," said the Wolf, focusing on his magazine.

"Hey, look, back problems run in my family!" Breca snapped. She thumped her bare feet on the cobblestone floor and bit her lip in pain. "Who decorated this place, anyway? Jack the Ripper?"

The Wolf threw his magazine at the wall opposite him. It slid to the floor helplessly.

"My sister, actually."

"Oh yeah?" said Breca, deflating.

"Yeah."

"Interesting."

"Yeah." He was waiting for her to say something else.

"Very interesting."

"Yeah."

"Huh." She was quiet for a minute. Then she said, "So, who cuts your hair?"

The Wolf growled. Breca smiled. She knew perfectly well that one of the rules of society, regardless of which world you're in, is that you never ask a bald man who cuts his hair.

"I mean, I was just wondering, so I could, you know, avoid going to them. Really. You should *sue*, Mr. Wolf."

Wolf sniffed aggressively.

"Are you *sure* you're not a lawyer? Cause you look like a lawyer. You're got the interrogative squint down *perfectly*."

Wolf stood up so quickly he knocked over his chair. He leaned into the bars and snapped
at Breca, "I am *not* a lawyer! I am the Queen's personal enforcer!"

"Uh-huh," said Breca slowly. "And what does a personal enforcer do, exactly?"

"Enforces!"

"Personally?"

"Sometimes!"

"Fascinating." She leaned back and crossed her legs. "So then, you're completely loyal to her Majesty, right?"

"Completely." The reply was curt and did not invite further discussion, but Breca was a two-year veteran of selling things on the phone, and as such a master of continuing dead-end conversations; she exercised her art with clinical precision.

"So this rumor I heard going round about the blood pact between your forefathers, when her ancestor beat yours at croquet— that you would always be the servants, and they ever the masters?"

She was winging it. Almost every royal family had some legend like this, in the books she read anyway, which was appropriate, and it was her own speculation as to why someone like the Wolf remained, apparently voluntarily, in the Queen's employ. But for all that, it got a reaction she hadn't expected.

The Wolf pulled the key from his pocket and opened the door. He did this very fast, and was inside the cell, moving on Breca far too fast for her to move aside. He swept her up, gripping her by the collar of her striped shirt, pulling her close to his face. Suddenly his eyes were much too large— they filled her vision with liquid gold, and his voice turned raspy and difficult to understand as though his vocal cords themselves were changing.

"Did you never wonder why I am called the Wolf?" he rasped.

To Breca's horror, his face began to lengthen, his ears and hair to grow. He snapped at her with those teeth.

— *those teeth—*

An expression of surprise crossed his face.

He dropped her and fell full-length onto the floor. Breca, realizing she hadn't actually been breathing whilst this was going on, gasped in air hurriedly, and looked from the Wolf's prone body up to Axford, who stood breathing heavily, the tracks of tears still on his face, and the fireplace poker still held in the air.

He dropped it with a clatter and ran to her, throwing his arms around her, shaking. He wasn't crying. He'd done that already. He'd finished with that.

"Are you okay?" he said in her ear.

"Are *you*?" she said. She was worried about the shaking. She patted his back, then wrapped her arms around him and held on, trying to stop it, hold him still.

"They killed the raven," he said. "The Queen—"

"What?" she said.

"The Queen hit it with a poker, and Death was there."

"Oh, Axford, I'm sorry."

He stayed still for a minute, then let go and straightened up. "Not as sorry as they're going to be. Let's go get some revenge," he said. He cast a careless glance down at the Wolf as he stepped past him.

"He was *actually* a wolf?" said Breca.

Axford shrugged. "You didn't know?"

She shook her head dumbly.

Axford took in a very deep breath. "Well, now you do. Okay, let's go."

"What, you're just going to leave him here?"

"What else do you suggest we do?"

"Well— we could put him in a cupboard—" She glanced around with a curious ineptness at the sparsely-furnished jail.

"Aren't you Miss Tidy," said Axford, somewhat savagely.

"I can't help it. Axford—"

"What?"

She hesitated for a moment, but only just. "Thank you."

He shook his head and refused to look at her. "Let's go." They clattered up the stone steps, steps mismatched, leaning on each other as much as they dared.

Death appeared in the darkness they left behind. "Interesting," he said. He nudged the inert Wolf with his foot. "Who knew the little man was so strong? Well, I did, obviously."

He stood and watched the body for a minute.

"Just as I thought," he declared suddenly. "Here this was supposed to be a vacation, and all of a sudden everybody wants a piece of the action. Er, inaction. Amazing, isn't it? They go their whole existence with no idea what death means, and then when I come along they turn it into a novelty, like prize bags, and start handing it out everywhere." He sighed and looked to one side, a little wistfully, then allowed his gaze to linger on the blackness for a minute before drifting back to the Wolf, who still hadn't moved. At all.

He sighed again. "Alright, well, but *you* deserved it."

A few minutes of industrious tugging had the Wolf stowed in the cupboard that Breca had helpfully pointed out shortly before. Death wiped something off his brow that some part of his brain registered as sweat. He patted the Wolf on the shoulder. "He could have just stolen your key, of course. I expect he didn't know you had one. Ah well. I'll deal with you later. You evil, *evil* man."

He closed the cupboard door firmly. "My Breca awaits. I assume."

The Breca that Death so blithely assumed was his strode down the corridor. Every bone in her body showed defiance, except for the ones in her hand, with which she gripped Axford's so hard that he gritted his teeth against the pain.

"Let's go," she said. "Let's get out of here, we'll go anywhere. I'd rather deal with Death than with your Queen and her entourage."

"She's not *my* Queen," said Axford.

"I mean, Death may not have any dignity, but at least he has some politeness. Some manners. Some honorable instincts."

"How do you figure?"

"Well— he's not just *taken* me like he could do. I mean, he's Death you know, not just some fellow with a crush on me. He's got an awful lot of power, and he hasn't used it at all. He's just tried to get me to go with him." She thought of the last few dream sessions there'd been. "He's had some pretty persuasive enticements, too."

"What?" Axford looked up sharply. "What exactly does *that* mean?"

She smacked him upside the head. "Not what you're thinking, clearly."

"How would you know what I'm thinking?" He rubbed his head resentfully. "But what do you mean by it?"

She sighed, folded her arms, and hesitated. "Oh, Axford, I'm homesick. He said if I came with him I could see my parents."

"You are *not* going with him."

She sighed. "Well, get me out of here, then. This place depresses me. It makes Death seem a perfectly reasonable alternative."

"Right. We'll go. I just have to—" He stopped, glanced around him, looked confused, said, "Excuse me a moment."

Then he went over to a nearby wall and said, "Do you suppose, since I *am* Axford Barrel the— ahem— *savior* of Wonderland, that you could help me out with the way to the Queen's suite?"

The wall said nothing.

Axford waited. Finally he stomped his foot and said, "Come on, I know you can talk!"

There was the sound of someone clearing their throat politely, and the wall said, "The Queen's sweet what?"

Axford frowned. The wall giggled.

"The Queen's *chambers.*"

"That sounds rather—"

"The Queen's *rooms*, which I suspect you knew the whole time."

"Oh, alright," said the wall, somewhat exasperated. "You're no fun anymore."

Axford folded his arms and tapped his foot. "I'm waiting."

"Take the left, then the right, then the left again, and you can't miss it. It's the big gold and purple door with a crown on it and vicious snores emerging from behind it."

"Thank you," said Axford curtly, and collected Breca.

Breca said, "What was *that* all about?"

"What? Oh. Well, it's a big castle. Er, I got lost, I had to ask directions."

"To *where*?"

"Oh, to the, er, the Queen's, er, rooms."

"What *for*?"

"For the key."

"What key?"

"The key to your cell."

"You could have just taken the Wolf's, you know."

"I didn't know he had one, did I? Anyway, I just have to put the key back."

"*What*? Axford, didn't you *steal* the key?"

"Yes." He sounded reluctant in answering, and indeed he was.

"Well, I should think you'd know this, dearest, but when you steal something *you don't put it back*!"

"You do if you're at all nice-mannered."

"Which you are not."

"Listen, Breca, if she wakes up and you're gone, but she still has the key, she'll think you managed it on your own, because nobody in their right mind would put the key back once they've stolen it, right? But if she finds it gone, she'll know I took it, and she will seek me out and do unspeakably nasty things to me."

"And if she wakes up and finds you in her room, she'll know you took it then, too."

"She won't find me in her room. She won't even wake up."

"How do you know?"

"I gave her a sleeping potion."

Breca paused, wondering where to go with that one. Did it even matter at this point, she thought, where on earth— where in Wonderland, rather— Axford had found the mickey to slip the Queen? She shook her head. "They wear off, you know."

"Which is why we're hurrying. Don't worry so much! Go with—"

"Axford, if you tell me to go with the flow, I'm going to slap you."

"Well, *don't* go with the flow then. But cool it anyway."

"This is a very bad idea," Breca maintained, but they were right outside the Queen's bedchamber now, and she hushed and stood tense as he slipped inside, clutching the key in his hand.

He tiptoed over to the bed, bent over the peacefully snoring Queen, slipped the key back on to the chain around her neck, and shrieked as someone grabbed him by the collar.

"Axford!' yelled Breca, running in and panicking rashly. "What the—"

"Alice?" said Prince Stoat, looking at her with bewilderment plain on his handsome, idiotic face. "What are you doing consorting with this— this ex-hero, petty thief?"

"He may be a petty thief," said Breca snappishly, "but he's *my* petty thief, isn't he?"

"That's right," said Axford, trying to twist out of Stoat's grasp. "I'm not even that petty, really."

"But— " said Stoat.

"And anyway he was helping me," said Breca. "What are *you* doing here?"

"Oh, I—" said the Prince, and looked embarrassed.

"Come on, out with it."

"Well, the Queen hired me to watch her room from the time she went to sleep till she woke up. She seemed to think she'd be burglarized." The Prince looked genuinely puzzled. "I can't imagine why."

"Where were you when I first got in, then?" demanded Axford. "You weren't here."

"Oh, well, she went to sleep rather early tonight— and, er— my watch was broken, so I—er— slipped out for a quick drink."

"Aha," said Axford. "You and everyone else."

"But you still haven't told me what you are doing here."

"Putting the key back, of course," said Axford. "I only borrowed it, after all. Let me go, will you?"

"What did you borrow it *for*?" said Stoat, who probably thought he was being immensely clever.

"To let me out," said Breca patiently. "See, your favorite Queen had me locked in the dungeons with a crazed Wolf-man."

"But— why?" Stoat's honest forehead wrinkled in perplexity.

"Well, it's a long story," said Breca with a sigh, "so I'm not going to bother explaining it to you. It's so early it's late— or is it the other way around? Yes, it is. Never mind that. Just let Axford go, and we'll let you be, alright?"

The Prince thought about this. "No," he said finally. "I don't see that I can do that without feeling tremendously guilty afterwards. The Queen and I have known each other since childhood, see, and even though I never really liked her all that much I still don't feel that I can let her down like this." He gestured vaguely, to indicate that if they didn't understand, they shouldn't sweat it. "It's a royalty thing."

"Oh, stop being such a gentleman, Stoat, and let him go."

"But— why?"

"This is getting tedious," said Death, stepping into the room. He gave Breca a careful smile. She responded to this by backing up till she was behind the Prince, who dropped Axford and stepped forward.

"See here," he exclaimed, "what do you think you're doing, sir?"

"Oh, shut up, Stoat," said Death, and added, "you're boring me." He flicked a finger at him, and the Prince clutched at his throat and reeled back into the wall, collapsing on the floor.

Breca shrieked wordlessly for a minute before she managed, "You killed him! You *killed* him! He was still all confused! I didn't get a chance to explain!" She dropped to her knees besides Stoat's prone body. "He's the only man who ever wanted to marry me! And he's still got that poor, confused, pathetic look on his face! And he's— oh, he's still breathing."

She looked up at Death, who shrugged.

"You didn't kill him, after all— well, that's all right then, um, er— " She patted Stoat's cheek, kissed him on the forehead, and stood back up.

"Nice day, isn't it?" remarked Axford, looking out the window.

"How did you know where to find me?" Breca asked Death.

"I kind of just followed the trail of chaos," Death answered, pointing a finger at Axford. "I thought about rescuing you myself, but I figured, no, let him have his moment of glory. He's really a very nice fellow, you know," he told Breca.

"Yes, I do know," said Breca, rubbing her eyes. "But how *you* know?"

"Oh. We met up at the pub. Shared a few, talked a bit." He gave a fondly reminiscent smile. "I rather enjoy it, this human socializing thing. It's much more agreeable than spending all my time either alone or in the company of dead people who, lets face it, aren't much for conversation."

"Oh, wow," said Breca, almost approvingly. "Incredible, isn't it? Male bonding rituals transcending time, space, and reality, and now Death is an alcoholic."

"Social drinker, at most. I wouldn't go that far."

"Well, I would," said Breca sharply. "I'll take every opportunity I can find to insult you. I'll look for openings on purpose."

"Oh, now, Breca," remonstrated Death, wounded.

"No, I mean it. I've always wanted someone I could be nasty mean to without feeling bad, and something tells me this is my chance. Listen, buster, if it weren't for the fact that you're nearly six feet tall, you'd be nothing but a slimy little creep. But you're taller than me, so that makes you a slimy *big* creep. And I'm not sure that's any better."

"Breca," said Axford, nudging her.

"Leave me alone, I'm trying to insult Death."

"Doing a bang-up job, too," said Death, trying not to laugh.

"Breca," said Axford again, nudging her harder and pointing at the bed. Death, too, turned to look and was soon staring at it.

The Queen was waking up.

"The night has just flown by, hasn't it?" said Axford with a grin.

It was, in fact, about eight o'clock in the morning, Wonderland time, and another gorgeous day. They didn't look at that, though. They watched the Queen's eyes fluttering, watched her reach up and scratch her head, watched her eyes open suddenly, watched her sit up like a shot, heard her yell, "What are you *doing* here?"

"Just watching you sleep," said Death, a faint smile tugging at the corners of his mouth.

"Alright for you," she said, "but what about *them*?"

Axford's mouth opened without asking permission first. "He was selling tickets," he said, pointing at Death.

"Upon my honor and everyone else's, milady," said Death formally, "I was not. No-one would buy any."

The Queen, with a show of regality that was completely unconvincing, got out of her bed, stepping over Stoat with only the merest of curious glances. She came to Breca, hands on her hips, sneered, and pushed her. Breca stumbled back, irritated, and gave the Queen a good shove in return.

"That's not fair!" yelped the Queen.

"Why not?"

"You lied to me! That merits a push! In fact it merits a great deal more than that!"

"When did I lie to you?" cried Breca, who was, for a moment, genuinely confused about this.

"You said you were Alice!"

Ah, there it was. She'd nearly forgotten. "Well— Axford lied to you first!"

"That doesn't matter!"

"Then quit making a fuss over it! Look, Your Majesty, I've been up all night, I've only got *one* nerve left, and you're getting on it!"

Somewhere on a faraway farm, a rooster crowed.

The Queen scrubbed her hands over her face, then stood suddenly still, with one hand over her eyes and the other creeping up to clutch at her hair.

Death stiffened and stood up straighter, his features sharpening visibly. There was something familiar about all of this, the Queen's stance, the look of things. He glanced carefully towards the bed, and smiled. Deathbeds still got him, after all this time—

A light, pleasant, feminine whisper resounded through the air.

Good morning, my lady.

The Queen took her hands down with a scream of rage. She stomped her foot and pointed a shaking, accusatory finger at Fred Death.

"You promised!" she shrieked, witchlike. "You *promised* me!"

Death gave a slow, very unpleasant smile. "I asked you if there was something you weren't telling me."

"*What?*"

"Had a little talk with two charming young women a bit before dinner. Do you know, there's nothing I can do about a previous contract?"

The Queen was rapidly turning green as the poison swam through her bloodstream. She gasped in pain and from her mouth poured a torrent of words— none of which were audible as Death picked her up and removed the breath from her lips.

She slumped over his shoulder.

He turned to look at Breca and Axford. "I'll be right back," he said, as he disappeared slowly into nothing. It sounded an awful lot like a promise.

"I could have told her that flirting with Death was a bad idea," said Breca, with a high, hysterical giggle. She was beginning to shake. "What was that all about, the previous contract thing?"

"I wonder," said Axford, supporting her as she collapsed, still giggling.

"Who does one sell one's soul to in Wonderland?" she asked as he let her gently down onto the floor.

He looked up at her blankly. "Beg pardon?"

"Do you?" she said, and chuckled. "Well, back at home, the less charitable among us would say she sold her soul to the Devil, to get to be Queen and all. But there's no Devil in Wonderland. Not now that she's gone." She smirked quietly to herself.

"Who indeed," said Axford, then suddenly overcome with a sense of purpose, gripped her hand and tried to pull her up. She was too big for him to have much effect on, but she yielded to his insistence and got herself up on her own steam.

"Where are we going?"

"Guess you'll find out, won't you."

She rapped him on the head. "Guess I will, little man."

He kicked her gently on the shin, ground his teeth, and led on.

Chapter Fifteen

Breca, wrapped in romantic cynicism, sat in the room outside the other room, in which her hero was conferring with the real, *real* rulers of Wonderland. She'd been there for ten minutes, and other than imagining scenarios in which Axford realized that he desperately needed her and told her so, she was utterly bored.

"Some waiting room this is," she said aloud. "Silent as the dead. Not even any three-year-old magazines."

She took her shoes off and examined her feet, then rolled her trouser-legs up and ran a finger from her ankles upwards to her knees.

She peered with interest at the pale gold hair on her forearms.

Then she stood, jumped up and down a bit, bent her knees slightly, and pretended to go wading at the seashore, which was *there* with a suddenness that frightened her. Seagulls screamed over her head and the silence was taken over by the roar and crash of the tide. A crab scuttled by at close range to her feet. She scrambled out of the cold water and onto her chair, tucking her feet up under her. She watched as the beach slowly faded out, replaced once again by the opposite wall of the long, low room, lined with chairs.

Breca had quite an imagination, but Wonderland was more than a match for her.

They'd again only been allowed in one at a time, so Axford went in first to try and jump-start his bravery.

He stood in front of the Twins and, politely, requested an explanation.

They looked at each other for a few wordless moments. Crosses stroked the Cheshire Cat, which sat on her lap and purred to itself.

"And that's another thing," said Axford. "How did that cat escape the Museum? Not that I go in there often, but I'm sure it was there the last time."

"When you think of the Cheshire Cat," questioned Crosses, "what's the first thing that comes to your mind?"

"The grin," said Axford. "It's the most noticeable thing about him. Apart from his basic cat-ness, anyhow."

"Precisely. So all people expect to see is a cat with all its teeth showing. What do you suppose we substituted?"

Axford thought. "Vampire?" he hazarded.

"Exactly. Now, people think vampires can only change into bats, but in fact they can take on nearly any animal form they wish. We found one that frequented a feline form, and had him cloned."

"So we've got a *vampire clone* in the museum?"

"Clones are people, too," said Noughts severely, "some of the time at any rate, and we made the bars extra strong anyway. Just as a precaution."

"Right," murmured Axford. "I'll have to go in and take another look at him. A closer look."

"Not too close," cautioned Crosses.

"Of course not."

Noughts leaned forward, a look of earnestness on her pale face. "If you want the truth, it's been years since any of the originals were in the Museum. How could we allow them to be cooped up so, when they were longing for freedom?"

Axford frowned thoughtfully. The March Hare, the Hatter, the other Queens and Kings, the Knights, the Lion and the Unicorn, Father William, the remains of Humpty Dumpty— "Where are they now?"

Crosses shrugged slight shoulders. "Free."

"And in the Museum, we have— counterfeits?"

"Only the best," they assured him. Axford shook his head, to put it forcibly out of his mind, and moved on.

"So what about the Queen then?"

The sisters sighed in unison. "When she came to us, she had a good sales pitch. She said she would turn Wonderland around. This was scarcely two years after Alice left, and in that time the situation had become intolerable. The Queen promised to change all that, promised many things. She seemed to be a good, honorable person who earnestly had Wonderland's happiness foremost in mind— we were completely taken in."

Noughts shrugged. "The woman was born a politician. What can we say?"

"At any rate we made her a deal. We would help her to be Queen, as long as she was ruling in the country's interest. To ensure this, if she failed to make things better, she would have a time trap. When she went to sleep, poison would—"

"Yes, I know that part. I saw it."

"And from then on it was a game. If she won, she kept her life. If not—"

"How did you know Death would show up?"

They exchanged glances.

"It's this Intuition thing," said Noughts. "It's a bit tricky sometimes, very difficult to explain fully—"

"Very complicated," Crosses assured him.

"So we weren't sure *how* it would happen."

"Just that it *would*."

"But we did our best."

"And it all worked out."

"So," said Axford slowly, "then, the Queen sending us to find Alice was—"

"Self-preservation," said Noughts quietly. "She knew the country needed something to come back to its best state."

"But she didn't know that all she needed was someone from Alice's world, not Alice herself," said Axford. "That's right, isn't it?"

"Yes, it is, Axford." Noughts smiled warmly at him.

"And so, Breca needs to stay," said Crosses. "You need to keep her here."

"I'll try," said Axford heavily. "Tell me how."

"Marry her," said Crosses.

"Yes, that would work," said Noughts thoughtfully.

Axford cleared his throat and decided to pass over that. "There's still the little deal with Death to sort out, though."

"Oh, that. That shouldn't be a problem."

"Tell me," insisted Axford.

"He is mortal, at the moment, and that is key. Far more mortal than we are, in the normal course of time."

"And that means that he can be killed."

"Not forever, you understand," Crosses hastened to clarify, "but it will send him back to Alice's world and prevent his coming back to Wonderland."

Axford shrugged. "That still is not telling me much. How do you suggest I go about killing him?"

Noughts, from somewhere Axford couldn't see, drew a long, glittering dagger, which the light shone off of in the traditionally accepted manner. Crosses, from presumably the same place, drew the scabbard, which was, as dictated by popular legend, covered in mystic runes which nobody could understand. They sheathed the dagger and presented it to Axford, who looked at it in bemused wonder.

"It's vorpal," offered Crosses, as though this were a telling feature. "Don't worry so much about it not being a sword."

"I, uh, don't have much, er, experience with this killing—" Axford said hesitantly.

"Plunge it into his heart," said Noughts.

"To the hilt," instructed Crosses, sorrowfully.

"Pointy end first," Noughts amended after a moment's thought.

Axford, half to himself, half for their benefit, ruminated, "Have to find a step-ladder somewhere—"

"Ah, the height issue. It's cursed you throughout your life, has it not? We've taken care of that," said Crosses. "Don't worry on that account."

"How, exactly?" Axford asked, a bit suspiciously.

"Just go now, and remember that no matter what else happens, the dagger must reach his heart."

Axford nodded and bowed his thanks deeply. He started towards the door but as he reached it, he turned and looked back at them.

"Do I take the scabbard off first, yes?" he said.

When Axford walked out of the Twin's room, Breca watched him with her mouth open and her eyes wide in something he could have sworn was pleased surprise. There was something odd about her, but at the moment he couldn't quite put his finger on it.

She jumped out of her seat and ran to him.

Oh, yes, that was it.

"Have you shrunk?" he asked her, tilting his head to one side quizzically.

"I don't *think* so. Axford, you're— well, not tall exactly, but taller than I am!"

"I am?" He looked down at his feet, which suddenly seemed a lot further away. Also the fact that he wasn't eye-to-navel with Breca was a bit of a giveaway as well. "I *am*! That's what they meant!"

"What who meant?"

"Well, they said they'd—" He gestured vaguely over his shoulder with his thumb and she interrupted him blithely.

"Oh, look, is it my turn? This is great, Axford, really great." She grinned at him as she went in the door, closing it firmly behind her.

"I get to save you now," he said aloud to the empty room, and grinned to himself. He shadowboxed for a few minutes. "Death, you are going down, down, down—" he said. He adopted a squeaky voice that sounded as like Death's as a whoopie cushion sounds like a Lear jet. "Oh no, no Axford, don't hurt me, please Mr. Barrel, I promise I'll be good, oh no, no— *pow! Whack! Boom!*"

The door opened and Breca came back out, a small, secret smile on her face. He was suddenly still, hands down at his sides, and his expression said *Who, me? I wasn't doing anything.*

"What'd they say?"

"Nothing I didn't already know," she answered serenely.

"Do I know it?"

"Not yet."

"Are you going to tell me?"

"Not now. What did they say to you?"

He gave her a sharp look, then said, "They told me how to defeat Death—"

"Oh, good."

"And save the country."

"Oh, wonderful. How?"

"For the first, they gave me this," he said, and turning to one side, stuck his leg out to showcase it and displayed to her the dagger. "It's vorpal."

"A vorpal— dagger?"

"Mm-hmm. Don't worry so much about it not being a sword, they said. Because he's mortal now, see, and that means he can be killed."

"I don't believe it for a moment," she said. "But you do, apparently, so that should be all right. And for the second?"

"And for the second? Well, saving you obviously has a great deal to do with it. And keeping you here. It's a representative of Alice's world that we need after all; so I suppose you could take off the wig."

She did, and tossed it in the corner, which caught it and with an elegant motion hung it on a previously nonexistent hat stand. "And what did they suggest for that?"

He hesitated, but only minutely. "They said I should marry you."

She laughed. "Did they."

"Yes." He frowned to himself. "I forgot to ask them exactly what that entailed."

"Oh yes." Breca rolled her eyes. "Do you think any of this will actually work, Axford?"

He hesitated, then sighed. "Truthfully? It's a matter of hope. Wishful thinking."

"And do you believe in miracles?"

"I believe in everything," said Axford. "It saves time."

She accepted this with a sage nod, as though to say she knew where he was coming from, and folded her arms. "So what do we do now?"

He shrugged. "Wait, I guess. It shouldn't be long."

"No?" They began to walk back up the corridor. "But I hate waiting."

"Would you like to go and look for him?"

"If you were at all a man, you'd go and look for him yourself."

"Don't you threaten me."

"I didn't."

"Oh."

They walked on. The castle corridors were still and silent, the morning rush over. No-one had found the Queen yet. They all thought she was having a bit of a lie-in, and were due to be pleasantly surprised as soon as the maid went to make up the bed and stir up the fire.

Breca looked down at her fingernails as though they merited close scientific observation. "Axford, this may sound silly, but— I'm scared to death of dying."

"Yes? You're right, that does sound silly."

"Well, I'm still scared."

"They say it's just like going to sleep."

"I'm afraid of that, too."

"How do you get anything *done*, Breca? You're afraid of everything."

"Not *usually*, I'm not. And I think I've done very well for someone who's had death after her for a week, and been locked up by a mad Queen, and almost drowned with someone named Stoat, and nearly had my head bitten off by a werewolf."

"Yes," he admitted. "You have done well."

"Really? You actually think so, Axford?"

"I do."

They walked on.

"Really?"

"How many times do you want me to say it, Breca?"

"Once more."

He pushed her. If he had been his regular size, it wouldn't have budged her, but as it was now, it shoved her none too gently into the wall. She rebounded into him with the force of it and punched him in retaliation.

"Sorry," he said, not greatly hurt by the punch since he'd warded it off with his hand.

"I'm not." Her voice was angry, but it made him laugh.

"Breca, you are— oh, so many things. Stubborn, headstrong, impossible to bring down. I mean *impossible*, even Death can't do it. That's quite incredible. You're good for my homeland. You're good for people, because even as you irritate them, you remind them that they're alive. That's a very nice quality. I admire it."

"Well, thank you very much, Axford Barrel. Coming from you that— that— makes me extremely angry."

She stomped ahead so hard the floor shook. Several steps behind, her prospective savior followed her with a wide grin on his upwardly mobile face.

Behind them, deep in the bowels of the castle, two sisters sang a sad and lonely tune.

"Moonlight on the lovers' way
"Behind the looking glass they say
"Their everlasting pledge
"Like hearts, does it quickly break
"Bits and pieces fastened make
"A cruel and jagged edge

"What's found is lost, what's lost is found
"What's done is done, and so
"They cannot stop when at the ground
"But bury far below

"Together down they fly beneath
"Into the secret deeps
"Lost to themselves, they trust the earth
"Their memory safely keeps

"An end to all; they heed no call
"Their final days have come to pass
"Their eyes close, blinded by the light
"Reflected in the looking glass."

Thankfully, it had as little to do with prophecy and reality as it did with meter and clarity. The sisters were just in a bit of a mood.

They waited. All through the afternoon, all through dinner, all through a fine old brandy afterwards from the Queen's private stock, and finally through Axford's announcement that it was bedtime. He waited outside the bathroom door as she changed into the white linen nightgown someone had found for her in the voluminous attic, and when she came out he hardly gave her a glance, but accompanied her in silence to her huge, five-walled bedroom, his eyes darting alertly to search out the depths of the corners.

She settled herself into the bed and tried to relax. It didn't seem to be working. Every muscle in her body was drawn tight as a taut bowstring.

"You think he'll come soon?"

"Haven't we been over this before?"

"Right. I'm sorry, Axford."

Axford pulled a chair over next to the bed and sat down in it with a great show of patience he didn't really feel. He fell asleep immediately. Breca watched him in disgruntled irritation, then leaned back against the pillows.

It seemed to take forever to get to sleep, but she managed, finally, somehow.

This time Death looked a little— she wasn't sure just what— happier, maybe.

"You feel the end coming on?" he asked.

"Yes."

"You know how this going to go?"

"Yes."

They were silent for a minute, looking at each other. "Are you thinking what I'm thinking?" he asked her.

"Oh, I hope not," she told him emphatically. "My life is complicated enough right now without sharing Death's thought processes."

"But we both think we know how it'll end."

"That may be so. In fact it is. But. How much do you want to bet that *my* ideal ending is different from *your* ideal ending?"

He shook his head. "Breca, Breca. I promise I wouldn't make you unhappy."

"No, you'd make me miserable," she agreed.

"You know why skulls grin, don't you, Breca? Because its only after death that you get the joke."

"That's great," said Breca, putting her hands on her hips. "That's great. Why don't you go off and become a really morbid comedian then?"

"Well, that's a bit of a drastic solution, isn't it?" Death looked put out.

"Look, death, I don't like to say that I don't enjoy our little chats every time I go to sleep, but, well, I don't. You're turning me into an insomniac, do you know that? I'm afraid to close my eyes any more. Even blinking makes me panic. It's awful, and I hate it. So how about giving me a break, okay? Okay?"

It wasn't till now that she noticed he had disappeared into the dark recesses of her mind. "Thank you," she said uncertainly. Only silence answered her. It made her unaccountably nervous. "Um— Death? Fred?"

At the sound of her tentative voice, her parents walked out of the darkness and stood looking at her.

"Mum? Dad? What are you doing here?" Homesickness flooded over her like an ocean. A lump rose in her throat and without much interval she began to cry, trying to catch it in her hands. The teardrops were enormous; they formed a puddle at her feet that gave her a glimpse into oblivion. She considered it.

Her mother smiled a sweet, sweet smile, and held out her arms. "Come with me, love. I'll take you home. Come with me."

"Yes," said Breca, forgetting Wonderland in an instant. "Yes, I will." She ran forward into her mother's arms, a little girl again, and had a brief moment of happiness, till her mother's comforting embrace turned into a much firmer, harder grip, and she looked up into Death's triumphant face. His eyes glittered.

"You said yes," he said.

Breca opened her mouth to scream.

"Would you stop that," said Axford, nudging her with his foot, which he had propped up on the bed. "I'm getting a bit tired of it, see. Breca?"

He moved to the side of the bed and sat down on it quickly, then felt her forehead. "You're terribly hot. Are you alright?"

She shook her head and gasped air. 'He's coming. He's coming—"

"Soon?" said Axford seriously.

"*Now.*"

He nodded and smoothed her hair. "It's alright. We're ready for him. Try to go back to sleep now. I'm right here."

"Yes, but where's the dagger?"

"I have it, I have it."

"Alright, then."

She sighed deeply as though emptying her lungs to the very depths, lay back and closed her eyes. Axford watched her exhausted face and went back to his chair. He cast glances to the five corners of the huge room and sighed.

At his waist the dagger waited.

Breca dreamed for a very long time of nothing except lying there awake in the cool room. She thought mistily of Axford and his worried eyes. After a long while, she became aware that even in her dream, her attention was focused on the door, which was closed, and didn't look as though it was about to be opened.

It was, though.

It opened, and Death came through it. Without hesitation, he walked over to her bed and stood besides it for a few moments, looking down at her. He knelt finally and said, "Wake up, Breca."

Breca opened her eyes and looked straight into those of Death.

"Oh, give me a break," she said.

"Hullo, Breca," said Death.

"It's you. I should have known."

"Well," said Death modestly, "you know what they say. Only two things you can count on in life: taxes and I."

"And me."

"No, me," said Death, confused.

"You said, 'taxes and I'. The correct grammar is 'taxes and me.'"

Death grinned, or grimaced; it was difficult to tell which was which. "I suppose that would be the third thing."

"What's that?"

"Contradiction."

She sat up and yawned, shaking herself. Now that the moment was here, it wasn't quite as bad as she'd been anticipating: arguing with Death like a pair of siblings wasn't nearly as terrifying as what she'd been picturing in her head. "This probably isn't good, right?"

"Oh, I don't know. That may depend upon your point of view.'

Like a pair of siblings, not that she'd ever had a sibling. Like an old married couple, she reminded herself, and shivered, wrapping her arms about herself. "So, it's true, then?"

"What is?"

"It really *is* all in how you look at it?"

Death grinned. "I think I'm going to enjoy eternity. How about you?"

"I don't know," she said frankly. "Eternity with Death? Sounds kind of boring, actually." She swung her feet over the edge of the bed and stood up. "Why isn't Axford waking up?"

"Heavy sleeper?" Death hazarded.

"You didn't put him out on purpose?"

"Nah. Where's the fun in that?" They stood and watched Axford together. "He's gotten taller, hasn't he?"

"Yes."

"Interesting." They stood a moment more, and Death observed, "He's not kidding when he closes his eyes, is he?"

"I shouldn't think so."

"Shall we wait for him to wake up so you can say goodbye?"

"Why wait?" said Breca, and gave Axford a good kick.

His eyes shot open and he leapt to his feet, taking in the situation in a series of glances and waving his arms in the air. "Right! Time has come! You can't take Breca, Fred, because Wonderland needs her!"

"Fred?" said Breca. "Seriously."

"Wonderland needs her, and, er, I need her, too!"

"Why?" enquired Death with cat-like curiosity.

"She makes me laugh!" bellowed Axford. "Not on purpose, admittedly, but— look, I'm taller now, so you can't terrorize me like you did last time! At least, not without considerably more effort, so I shouldn't advise it!"

"I didn't terrorize you last time," Death reminded.

"Time before that, then!"

"Time before that, I got drunk with you, remember? And I bought all the drinks!"

"Right! Well! You can't terrorize me at all, then! Hah! Terrorism is a trend you will not be setting!"

"Axford," said Breca, "why are you shouting like a drill sergeant?"

"Oh, was I shouting? Terribly sorry, I, er, have water in my ear." Axford shook his head violently, blushing a little. "Sorry."

Death, however, was focused on something else. He pointed at Axford's waist. "What is that?"

Axford looked down, said, "Oh! Right!" and unsheathed the dagger. "I almost forgot. I'm to fight you. For Breca. For the good of the country. For the good of Breca and the country!"

Death shook his head. "Axford, I didn't expect you to be in on this patriotism thing. It's absolutely rampant where I come from, but I didn't think it had spread this far. So you're going to fight me for Breca, hmm? Right. You do remember that I'm *Death*, right? Right. Well, alright, if you insist—"

He put his hands up in a sort of pseudo-judo, then stopped and snapped his fingers. "Oh, that's right, with all the excitement I nearly forgot. I was expecting something like this, and I, er, brought some friends."

Two huge black dogs with fierce red eyes and razor-sharp fangs emerged from the shadows and advanced, grinning. Axford yelped and tried to back away, but the dogs drew great breaths and from the mouth of one shot fire, from the mouth of the other, ice. The flame and the freeze traveled together, working in common, until there was, finally, a wall of thick, clear ice, cold and hard and smooth as glass, surrounding Axford and the dogs, excluding them from everyone else. A combat room, with Death and Breca as the onlookers, on the other side.

"A combat room," said Death, rather proudly.

"But I'm not any good at combat!" wailed Axford.

Breca ran forward, shouting his name, but fetched up at the wall and, though she met her on the other side, they could not break through.

Then the dogs advanced, and Breca got a good look at them. There was only one word for anything that diabolical.

"Hell-hounds!" breathed Breca.

Only one *hyphenated* word.

Death, however, laughed. "Oh, for heaven's sake, woman. As if I'd have those things in my house. And anyway there's no such thing as Hell, at least not the type you're thinking of. *I* told you that. Those are the Queen's dogs. Ex-Queen's," he added with a fiendish grin.

And then he stepped forward.

Axford held up his hands in as much of a placatory gesture as he could manage. Years of unused placating was going into his hands now. He thought the urgency of the situation warranted it. He had a feeling that it would be difficult to emerge from this room alive, and that worried him. Even with his new height, the hounds were still quite as big as he was. "Now, look, guys. Now look. I don't want to fight. Do you honestly want to fight someone who doesn't want to fight?"

The dogs couldn't speak, but the answer was, apparently, yes—

"Come with me, Breca."

"No."

"*Please* come."

"I won't! You're *Death*, and I won't go willingly no matter what you do!"

Breca had moved away from the wall to make her point, right in Death's face. Getting a good look at his expression, she now took a step back.

"You said yes once, not that long ago," Death reminded her.

"That was in a dream," Breca whispered. "And false advertising."

"You forget where you are. Dreams are just as real as waking, here."

"Well, anyway it makes no difference," she went on, mustering up some bravado. "Haven't you ever heard the song *Things Have Changed*?"

His face took on the listening look that meant he was going through his vast memory, piece by piece, very quickly. "Maybe," he said. "I'm not sure. Sing it to me."

Breca sighed.

"*Things have changed,*" she sang, nearly tuneless. "*Things have changed/ things have changed now/ da da da/ oh yeah they've changed/ things have changed/ boom boom/ things have changed/ things were things and now they're different, things have really changed now/ things have changed changed changed changed.*"

There was a slight pause. It took most of the courage Breca had to smile cheerfully at him.

The man with Fred's face and Fred's sense of humor smiled back, and said, "You made that up."

"I made that up," she agreed.

He took another step forward.

"Ever heard the song *Kiss of Death*?" he asked quietly. "I could sing it for you."

Breca felt the cold hard wall against her back and knew that she had nowhere to go. Even if she ran, he would only follow, and the pattern would repeat, endlessly and forever. She looked up at him and was caught off guard by the human in his eyes.

"You really are—"

"I am."

She pushed the cowl back off his head and saw the thin, wiry hair, the shadow of his cheekbones, the fine, clean lines of the skull beneath the skin.

"Wow," she said, frankly, and he moved closer then before she could get her defenses up again.

He put a hand up, wonderingly, to her throat, and felt her pulse. "Your heart is beating far too fast," he told her, "you'd better be careful," and kissed her. His fingers, though they brushed her skin lightly, left bruises blossoming under them.

She began to fall, but he caught her before she got too far.

Axford, already heaving for breath and covered with a lot of sweat and a little blood, caught in his losing battle with the Queen's watchdogs, looked through the ice and saw Death, Breca draped across his arms. Death saw him, too, and smiled as he turned away.

Axford ran at the wall, howling her name at the top of his voice. The dogs growled and leapt at him together.

He ducked.

They sailed over his head and crashed through the wall, shattering it into diamond-hard, needle-sharp shards. A few rolls through that and they were forever still.

Axford struggled to his feet and beheld Death. The shards had reached him as well, and the robes hung in tatters over his shoulders. They had been no good for protecting his skin, and it, too, had been cut.

He laid Breca down, carefully, then stood still, half bent, staring transfixed at the blood that came from the cuts on his hands.

"What?" he said. "What— is that?"

"Blood," said Axford, matter of factly, and shrugged.

"Blood," said Death. "*Blood*?"

"Oh, come off it, Fred," said Axford. "Don't tell me that, in your profession, you've never seen blood."

"My," said Death, lifting his hands towards the light, turning them this way and that. "*Oh, my.*"

Axford suddenly realized what he'd done, and a half-crazed laugh escaped him.

Death got very angry. He looked from a tentatively-triumphant Axford to his own borrowed body, which was beginning to fade out, going somewhere other than Wonderland regardless of how he felt about it.

"I'm dead!" he cried. "I'm Death, and I'm dead! You *killed* me and now I'm *dead!*"

"Really? Thanks for telling me," said Axford. "I wasn't sure."

Death, or the part of him that was left, anyway, gave a wild, eldritch howl of ancient frustration and leapt for Axford, who jumped to one side, still chuckling, and almost as an afterthought, plunged his dagger into Death's heart, to the hilt.

"I killed Death!" he said, and did an insane little dance, waving his bloody hands in the air, grinning wildly at the ceiling. He nearly tripped over Death's outstretched arm; he had fallen, full-length across the floor, and as he was disappearing from sight with his last strength he was reaching for Breca.

She opened her eyes in time to meet his gaze as he was swallowed up by air. Then he was gone.

Axford hurried over to Breca where she lay slumped on the floor. Her eyes were open and she blinked slowly as his head hove into view.

"Breca—" he said. He helped her to sit up. She pointed a crooked finger at where Death had been and made a small sound, somewhere between a mew and a squeak.

"He's gone," he told her, "he's gone, alright?"

She swallowed a few times, hard, and Axford traced the outline of her chin, trying to help her speak and not knowing how. "He's just gone back to my world, you know," she managed at last, her voice hoarse. "Just because no one will die in Wonderland doesn't mean all mankind is safe."

Axford tried not to glare at her. "You do take all the fun out of things," he said, squinting at her. "I'm trying to be all triumphant and heroic and that, and you bring me back to reality with a thump. It's not very grateful of you, is it? And not at all what I deserve. I just saved your life, you know."

"Yes, I know." Her voice was very soft, much quieter than he'd ever heard it before. This worried him. He looked in her eyes, to make sure they were clear, but his gaze was drawn to the purple and yellow bruises that Death's touch had left on her throat. He touched them with a careful fingertip.

She laughed, or tried to laugh, but she'd been crying, was still crying, so it sounded rather strangled. "Think they'll ever go away?"

The panic tears that had been lurking behind Axford's eyes finally overflowed. He kissed her cheek, her forehead, pulled her head down on his shoulder and smoothed her hair, and held her while she wept.

"They'll go away," he told her. "Eventually. It may take some time; but time is what you've got."

"I don't know," said Breca. "Sometimes I wonder—"

The room was empty, except for them, and they sat still a little longer.

Chapter Sixteen

The next thing of any importance that occurred was that the peasants got fed up and stormed the castle.

Breca got out of bed when she heard the screaming and yelling, joined Axford on the balcony, then pushed him out of the way. She held up her hands for silence. It took about fifteen minutes, but she got it.

Then she began to speak, and though it wasn't mesmerizing as the old Alice had been, there was still a certain something. People listened.

"I understand that you heard that my name is not Alice. That is correct. My name is Breca Marie Sigh, believe it or not, and I have come here somewhat under false pretenses— but hear me out. Your Queen told you that if Alice came back, everything would go back to the good old years. Well, listen! Nothing ever goes back to the way it was. Time has a sense of self-preservation, just as people do. Its important to keep things going forward. The nice thing about the future is that things can get better than they were in the past. The past never changes. It's only in the future that there's any room for improvement. But your Queen told you part of the truth. In order to get better, Wonderland does need someone from Alice's world. That *is* where I'm from."

She paused a moment to see how everyone was taking it. There were murmurs in the crowd, but they were quiet murmurs. Quite different from the dull angry roar of a few moments ago. Breca straightened her shoulders.

"So you really only have one choice," she said. "Accept me the way you accepted Alice. Don't forget her, don't ever forget her. But remember me, too, make room for me— Breca in Wonderland. Move with me into the future." She bowed her head, stepped back and smiled peacefully at Axford. "Done my duty now. I think I have a future in politics."

"Don't let the—" Axford bit his tongue. "The raven wouldn't have liked to hear that," he finished quietly. Breca put a hand on his shoulder, and he patted her. "So. You're staying, then?"

"You bet I'm staying. Wouldn't miss it for the world. Well, my world, anyway."

Axford smiled. The smile turned to a grin, the grin to a chuckle, the chuckle to a laugh.

"What?" Breca asked, baffled. "What's funny?"

"Not funny. Just odd."

"What is it?"

"I don't know." He shook his head in some wonderment, put a hand up to feel his own dimple. "Suddenly— everything's alright."

"Alright?"

He smiled again. "Okay."

She thought about this and then she began to smile as well. "An interesting concept."

"Yeah."

"It may take some getting used to."

"Well, we've got forever, haven't we?"

Much later, just before sunset, they sat together, shoulder to shoulder, on the lawn at the back of the palace. In the distance, there was a hubbub happening.

"What's all that about?"

Axford stood up and squinted into the distance. "There seems to be a giant blue hamster stuck in the storm drain."

"Coming or going?"

"Coming, it looks like."

"Probably someone's pet." She tugged his hand till he sat back down again. "And so?"

"And so?" echoed Axford. He rubbed his eyes and yawned. "I don't like the sound of that *and so*. Listen, young lady, I've had a hard week, killing Death, saving the country and all. What do you expect me to do now, play a quick game of Ping-Pong before I stumble off to bed?"

"Well, no," said Breca reproachfully, "but a kiss would be nice."

"A kiss," Axford repeated.

"Yes."

"Didn't you, er, get one of those from some other guy, earlier on?"

"That's why I desperately need one from someone I actually *like*. To get the taste out of my mouth. As it were."

Axford thought about this, and laughed.

"Breca, if anything ever gets you down, if you're ever seriously depressed, and I'll probably never see the day that it'll happen— if it does come, I may just have to hang myself and have done."

"It probably wouldn't work. You'd probably just have a new really *avant garde* necklace."

"Probably not. Great, isn't it."

"Sure. Anyway—"

"Oh, sorry, didn't mean to change the subject." Although he had meant to, of course. He was disappointed it wasn't working.

"Axford, that's what they told me."

"What are you talking about?"

"The Twins, when I was in the room with them. Remember I said I'd tell you about it later? They told me I was most likely in love with you." She watched him eagerly. "Like I said, nothing I didn't already know."

Axford shook his head. "Listen, Breca, I don't like to have to tell you this, but— I'm afraid you're the wrong way round as regards our relationship."

Breca's cautious, sheepish smile faded. A look of puzzlement and then one of apprehension crossed her face. "What?"

"Well—I've always looked on you as—more a sort of—sister, really."

Her eyes widened and her face froze. Shock, disappointment, and anger were clearly visible there, along with a cold and evident desire to commit murder that, sadly, she was unable to do anything about. If she tried, he would just laugh. She shoved her chair back in all haste, got to her feet with an immense remoteness and began to move away.

He watched her a few minutes to see what she would do. Her actions appeared to be limited to walking away as quickly as possible.

So he got to his feet and chased after her.

"Breca— Breca— come back here."

She was too far gone to hear.

Winston was a farmer, and a good one at that. A sun-browned and steady man of sixty, he was made for it. He possessed an unchangeable and time-weathered nature, and more than a passing resemblance to a rock. He plowed his field with a dedication that would have been appreciated in any elected official, and listened to the weather reports on the tinny old radio perched on the back of his seat.

He had his back turned when a figure fell out of the broad blue sky, followed by an object that flashed in the sun. The tractor was purring loudly, so he didn't hear the thump when the figure hit the ground.

On the next pass down the cornfield, though, he ran over the leg of a man he knew. Not in the least surprised by this development, he choked the tractor and clambered down to see if he was going to be sued out of ten years' crop.

To his surprise, Fred didn't even wake up. And the leg, which should have been mangled and flattened and useless, was just fine.

Fred simply lay there, effortlessly, easily, a slight, puzzled smile on his face. He was wrapped in what looked to Winston like an old blanket— though he couldn't understand why it was so dark. His wife made blankets. They were all brightly, sometimes offensively, colored. They were made of patches of old undergarments and someone else's clothes. He approved of this, with the incurious certainty of one of his cows, as being the way things should be. But this— who would want a dusty black blanket?

He couldn't figure out what Fred was doing in his cornfield, either. Sure, and lots of things had supposedly been found in cornfields. But Fred Killjoy? Perhaps— he studied the smile on Fred's face. Perhaps. Perhaps not.

He shook his head and prodded Fred with his boot.

Fred opened his eyes. Had the farmer had been marginally more perceptive, he'd have taken a step back.

"Where am I ?" said Death.

"In ma cornfield," grunted Winston. "What harpened ter yer, Fred?"

Death stood up, and took a look around him, and sighed.

"I lost," he said, scratching his head with one hand and putting the other on his hips. He continued to regard the landscape in a fairly disdainful manner.

"Eh?"

"Strangely enough, though, it's good to be home."

The farmer looked around him, doubtfully.

"Is ert?"

"Yes, my friend," said Death, "it is indeed." He flicked his gaze back to Winston, lifted his left hand, and nudged towards him experimentally.

The farmer's eyes rolled back into his head and his knees buckled—

"Aha," said Death, steadying him. "Just wanted to be sure."

Winston blinked at him. A sort of fear began to enter him, which he most certainly wasn't accustomed to.

"Well then," said Death, and he smiled. "That's all right. That," he added in satisfaction, "is just fine."

He smiled and was gone. The color flooded back into him as a confused, half-addled Fred Killjoy left limbo and returned to himself and found that he was inexplicably in Winston MacGregor's cornfield.

"How'd I get here?" he roared.

The farmer backed away hurriedly. Fred Killjoy shook his head, lifted a hand and scrubbed at his hair, found he was wearing a black robe and cowl, ripped it off, and began to stumble out of the cornfield in his Union Jack boxer shorts.

A little farther on, the farmer found the sickle. He ran over it, too, with the tractor, and wasn't the least bit surprised to find that it hadn't been affected at all. He bent to pick it up, straightened, sighted along the edge. In the unaccustomed spirit of curiosity, he swept it along the line of corn in front of him. It went cleanly through, but the corn stayed put. It stayed, as it were, stalk still.

"Hmm," said the farmer, ruminatively. "Dull as dishwater." And with a feeling of queasiness, of wanting to get it away from him, he flung it high into the air, as far from him as he could get it.

An invisible hand was put out to catch it.

An inaudible voice said, *Thanks very much, old man.*

Death still reigned. On our world, anyway.

The sun was setting on Wonderland's landscape, revealing unexpected mountain ranges and a distant glimmer as if from untold seas. The sky had turned from blue to pink and gold, everything bathed in a royal light.

The land had the qualities that usually come after a good rainstorm has washed away all the wrong and the bad and the generally naughty. If Wonderland had a face, it would be asleep, and smiling gently at its dreams.

In the Museum, irritable and quite, quite bored creatures were being let out to freedom once more—

—while elsewhere, heads that knew the truth lifted, listened, then smiled and breathed out in relief—

—while a Prince chucked it all and headed to the pub to meet the bartender—

—while a large white rabbit pulled out his ceremonial watch, looked at it, shook his head worriedly, jiggled the watch three times fast, and dipped it in the butter nearby—

—while deep underneath the peaceful soil, two girls abandoned their dignified postures and gave each other identical grins—

—while a large cat chased a small dog around the castle above—

—while in other worlds, other times, the definition of happiness was how close you were to the one you love, so stranger's eyes met across a crowded room and rhapsodized together with no words exchanged, and so there was peace for the terminally shy—

—while here in Wonderland, a hand reached out to take possession of another.

"I was only joking."

"Axford, I hate you."

Because all truth is concealed beneath layers of untruth, and if you scrape dedicatedly away at reality you'll find that you can't ever really know the difference, you can't ever really know anyone, least of all your own self, and you'll always be *wondering*—

And the fun part is finding out that it doesn't really matter.

Without Alice

Alice's Adventures in a Demi-Hell

A Short Story Not Set In Wonderland

Alice opened the door in response to a not-quite-timid knock and found no one, but mushrooms flowering in brilliant and unexpected splendor on her front lawn. She gave them a narrow glance, suspicious at once but vaguely so, and looked around a moment more for the invisible knocker who was, as the term implied, nowhere to be seen; then she went back inside, closing the door with care and precision.

She returned to the kitchen and resumed cracking eggs into a large bowl. The canister of flour was next, large and cold tin handed down from wartime and nutrient pinching and food stamps; she grappled with it gamely for a moment, her small hand on the large lid scrabbling for purchase.

"May I help you with that?" asked a pleasant voice.

She handed it over willingly, frowning still at the recipe on the counter before her. "I wish you would," she said a bit petulantly. "It is so hard to do when one's hands are too small."

"Perhaps you should make them grow," opined the voice.

"Perhaps I should," she agreed, "though it would take some convincing."

"Persuade them."

"I may try," she murmured, distracted by the vagaries of the print, and the voice was stricter this time.

"Don't *mutter* so, child. The only person who can hear you is *you*, and no one ever got any benefit from talking to themselves. You only ever tell yourself what you want to hear, and that is nothing but tickling your own ears."

Alice realized suddenly that there was something strange about this voice— it was quite muffled-sounding, for one, and for another, it should not have been in her kitchen, as she lived alone. She whirled about to find a knight standing there, bent slightly forward in a solicitous manner.

"Why are you here?" pleaded Alice, quite alarmed. The knight took a step back and cocked his head to one side.

"To be sure, I am not sure," he declared. "But that, like me, is neither here nor there."

Alice squinted at him. "You look quite familiar. May I see your face?"

"May you? *Can* you? Most certainly you may, though I do not know if you can." The knight lifted his visor, revealing a wizened, kindly face with decorative whiskers. "Best to ask both questions, and be thorough," he advised her. "Then there is little room for confusion."

There came a chorus of mismatched voices from Alice's living room. "No room! No room!"

"And when there is a little," said the knight obliviously, "you can always make more."

Alice gave him a narrow-eyed, suspicious look, which he promptly and with enthusiasm responded to by sticking his tongue out; a move which he no doubt regretted as the cover of his helmet, responding to the inexorable law of gravity, slammed down onto it. He gave a yelp and was sheepishly silent.

"Let that teach you to be rude," said Alice severely, shaking a flour-covered finger at him.

"But suppose he already knows how?" piped an inquisitive voice from the living room. Turning about, she beheld a furry, snub-nosed face peering in at the corner of the door. As she watched, the nose twitched. "Suppose he's already learnt," the Hare repeated thoughtfully. "What then?"

"Are you implying," came another voice, equally as familiar and equally as strange, "that a thing, once learnt, can never be unlearnt and, perhaps, re-learnt? Or that this arguably unknowledgeable man—" The Hatter sidled through the doorway and approached the knight, gesturing towards him airily. "This man who may or may not have learnt— that remains to be seen— and tell me true, does this man look to be learnt at all, or does he not, rather, look like an impressive idiot?" He stopped speaking, leaving half-completed sentences littered around him on the floor like gumdrops, and stared rather hard at Alice; clearly despite, the other questions that had come before, *this* was the one meant to be answered.

"*I* would never say anything so rude," said Alice, with dignity, folding her arms and looking aloof. The Hatter stared twice as hard and released a crooked smile, at which Alice blushed. "Well, *have* I ever? I would expect you to know, having said rude things quite often."

"Have not!" cried the Hatter, upset.

"Have so," retorted Alice.

"Did not, do not, can not, will not," recited the Hatter rapidly, and folded his arms with a flounce.

"That's beside the point," said Alice. "*I* would never do it. Or— say it, rather."

"Perhaps *you* need to learn," said the Hare with a certain desultory weariness, and shook his head.

"What are you all doing in my house?" enquired Alice, following the group as they turned and went back into the living room.

"You opened the door," said the Hatter severely. "We had only to knock."

"But I saw no one out there!"

"That's hardly my fault, is it?" the Hatter point out crisply, and seated himself rather proprietarily on the sofa.

"Perhaps you weren't looking hard enough," suggested the Hare.

"I looked quite as hard as I could," objected Alice, exchanging another glare with the Hatter, who looked affronted at her temerity.

"Perhaps," said the Hare again, "you should learn to look harder. It may take some effort, and building up the muscles. Carrots, I believe, are supposed to be good for your eyes."

The Hatter leapt up, as if stung. "*Carrots!*" he cried

plaintively. "*Are* they? Are they, you inconsiderate beast? Going on about carrots— all the *time* he's yammering on and on about carrots and their medicinal properties. Well, I ask you—" He turned to Alice with ferocious extravagance of motion. "What would you say to someone who's obsessed with vegetables?" As soon as she opened her mouth, he lifted both hands in a cease-and-desist gesture and bellowed, "Not yet! I'll be right back!" He dashed out of the room. Alice blinked once, twice, and turned back to the remaining creatures.

"I was only going to say, you being a Hare after all, perhaps it wasn't *too* strange—"

"Oh, certainly," said the Hare, flopping its ears over its head with irritation, "typecasting. Typical."

"I didn't intend any offense, I'm sure." Alice seated herself on the sofa and smoothed her apron over her knees.

"Perhaps you'll think about it before you open your mouth next time," said the Hare sharply, as the Hatter rushed back in and began jabbing at the Hare's eyes with two carrots appropriated from Alice's icebox.

"Good for the eyes, are they? ARE THEY?"

The Hare yelped and fended the infuriated little man off. "Steady on!"

Alice crossed her arms and directed a withering glare at the frantic Hatter, which did no good whatsoever as he did not turn to receive it. So she uncrossed them at once, and stood and strode to them, and took the carrots decisively from the Hatter's hands. He collapsed at once, subdued and sheepish. "That's quite enough," Alice told him severely. "How would you like it if someone did that to you? I daresay you'd have a thing or two to say about it!"

"I would," said the Hatter airily, losing his sheepishness and straightening up at once. "I'd say, 'Excuse me, would you kindly remove your vegetable from my eye? It's markedly uncomfortable.' And then I'd say, 'Nice weather for it, isn't it—'"

"Nice weather for what?" demanded the Hare. The Hatter shrugged expansively.

"Whatever you like," he allowed, with generosity of spirit. "What would you say?"

"Nice weather for sticking carrots in people's eyes?" snapped the Hare, with as much cunning as he could manage, and the Hatter brightened considerably.

"Yes, I thought so myself," he said, pleased, and attempted

to resume said activity; but Alice held the carrots behind her back. In the ensuing undignified struggle, the Hatter's hat got knocked off; it fell to the floor and the Dormouse rolled out, gasping for breath.

"Thought I was going to die!" it voiced at the top of its squeak. The Hatter looked down at it disdainfully.

"Well, you're not."

"Ah," said the Dormouse, relieved, "that's alright then," and it closed its eyes and began to snore. The Hatter rolled it back into the hat with his foot, then clapped it back on his head grimly.

Alice had taken advantage of this distraction to sneak back into the kitchen and replace the carrots in the crisper; the knight looked up from paring potatoes with his fingernails and gave her a sympathetic look.

"What are you doing?" she asked, though she was almost afraid to. The knight looked back down at his task and frowned thoughtfully.

"I am either freeing the unfortunate souls of these tubers from their mortal jackets, thus enabling them to live in everlasting whiteness, or I am making stew."

"Perhaps I'd better go back out to the living room," said Alice, wisely. She suited action to plan at once, returning just in time see the Hare struggling to pull the Hatter's topper down over his eyes. The Hare was seething, the Hatter yelping and putting up a fight, and from inside the maltreated article of haberdashery came a kind of terrified snore. Alice rushed over, pushed the Hare out of the way, removed the Hatter's hat and the dormouse from it, and placed the small sleeping creature on top of the piano where it was out of harm's way. Then, ignoring the look of triumphant vindication the Hatter was giving her, as though she owed him something and had finally paid up, she handed the topper back to the Hare.

"As you were," she said.

She left the room to the sounds of battle, and sought sanctuary down the hall. She opened the bedroom door to discover a terrified maid with a baby in her arms, frantically kicking at the walls.

"What?" cried Alice, rushing in. "What's wrong?"

"Can't get *out*!" cried the maid. "Can't get *out*!"

"Let me help you," said Alice, soothingly, calling on her two years experience teaching children in the first form to lend the right tone to her voice. The maid turned a rather quizzical look on her.

"Thank you," she said, politely, "but I'm doing just fine." And she redoubled her efforts, kicking at the walls so hard that even her soft-soled shoes left marks and dents. Alice hesitated, unsure of what to do; but the maid was determined, and the baby was squalling, so Alice chose the better part of valor and withdrew, leaving the door open behind her. The maid was working her way round towards it, at any rate, and would undoubtedly discover the opening eventually; though not, it seemed, before Alice's walls were stoved in beyond easy repair. That was part of the trouble with houses, Alice thought— if she didn't have the cottage, she wouldn't have to worry about the state of its walls. Then again, if she didn't have the cottage, she would have to be concerned with keeping herself dry, especially now, in the rainy season. Perhaps that was why the mushrooms popped up so suddenly, she reasoned. All the dew-wet ground.

This gave her an idea, and she turned about and walked back towards the living room and the front door. Passing the kitchen, she poked her head through the doorway to see that the knight had not injured himself with his fingernails or, alternately, the potatoes; he appeared to be well and happy, however, working away now at peeling a stalk of celery, string by string. Alice reckoned that this was less dangerous than the other, and left him to his own devices.

The Hatter and the Hare were now staring at each other balefully over cups kidnapped from her kitchen; there was no tea in them, at present, but this didn't seem to stop them from sipping defiantly from them every so often. She walked quickly and quietly through the room and slipped outside the front door.

It was cool still out there, even as the morning wended along towards early afternoon, and she walked in the sunshine, discovering flour on her hands and arms and wiping it away with her apron. The mushrooms were brilliantly colored, scattered haphazard around the lawn and encroaching on her garden; she spied a particularly large one and walked towards it, positive that she was at last headed in the right direction.

Indeed, the large mushroom led to a larger one, and the larger one to an even larger one, and so on and so forth until, with a distinct feeling of *deja vu*, Alice found herself circling around the tree-wide white trunk of an absolutely enormous one, looking up two feet over her head to the umbrella spreading of the dark red cap. She could not see anyone or anything up there: the cap mounded upwards a considerable height. She considered for a moment, then knocked politely on the smooth trunk. It was spongy and cool under her knuckles.

"Who's *there*?" came the voice that she was expecting. Alice smiled a little.

"I am," she said. "Who's there?"

"*I* am," said the voice irritably. "And if, as I take it to mean, this does in*deed* signify that once again I am conducting a conversation with myself, I object to my choice of time. I was in the midst of very deep meditation. Or," the voice added after a moment, "possibly mediation. Yes, in fact I *was* in *very* deep mediation."

"Between who, or what?" asked Alice, confused.

"Between Who *and* What," snapped the voice. "They're fighting again. They're always fighting. Who insists that What is incorrigibly rude, and What insists that Who gets all the respect among grammartarians. I was just after telling them that we're all capitalized here, and there need be no prejudice, but then Whom had to stick *his* nose in and inform Who that she was low-class and common. Who responded badly, I'm afraid, by telling her cousin that he was only in proper use *part* of the time, and reflected poorly on his sentences when his employers used him in misguided attempts to sound *posh*."

"Oh my," said Alice, smiling despite all this. "It sounds a dreadful row. Is it possible that I might beg a bit of your time, however, in between all this mediation?"

The voice paused. Then, "Come on up here, child," it said.

Alice went back to the beginning of path of mushrooms, and climbed atop the first one. Then, working her way slowly and with care, she made it up the increasing fungus stair-steps, one by one, until she reached the highest point; whereon sat the caterpillar, resplendent in state, reclining languorously and doing needlepoint.

Alice stood and laughed a little, breathless from the climb.

"I thought you had turned into a butterfly!" she said.

"What a ridiculous suggestion," said the caterpillar imperturbably, making another pass with the needle and thread.

"It's not, you know," said Alice candidly. She got to her knees carefully, and sat there to speak with him a while. "It isn't at all ridiculous to expect a caterpillar to turn into a butterfly. It's the sort of thing that happens all the time."

"Would it be ridiculous," inquired the caterpillar with frosty dignity, "to expect a spanner to turn into a corkscrew? Or a cake to become a full-course turkey dinner for two? Or a donkey to take the form of a human female and make rude remarks?"

"Well, yes," Alice admitted. "That would be most unusual."

"Hmm," said the caterpillar, squinting at her meaningfully. Alice sat very straight.

"I'm sure I don't know what you mean," she said.

"Hmm," said the caterpillar again. "I suppose if I told you I expected you to be taller, you'd insist I was being rude, would you?"

"I think you want me to say yes," said Alice, "but in all truthfulness I have to say no. Oh dear—"

The caterpillar jumped; he had stabbed himself in the finger with his needle. As he attempted to lift the square of cloth away, it was discovered that he'd sewn it to his sleeve and was therefore unable to successfully extricate himself. He glared at Alice and dropped the cloth to dangle like a handkerchief from his wrist.

"Now see what you've done," said the caterpillar.

"Me?" repeated Alice, trying not to laugh. "But I'm terrible at sewing!"

"Exactly," said the creature, with determination. Alice shook her head.

"I've only come to ask what you're all doing here. I don't wish to be rude, but the last thing I expected was abrupt houseguests. I *was* in the middle of baking. And after all this time, it's quite a surprise—" She turned as she was speaking, and caught sight of something that made her quieten. The view from the top of the mushroom, some ten feet off the ground, was more spectacular than she realized. Her lawn and garden laid out neatly, her small trim cottage on the other side of the greenery, and to the right, the grand slope of field that led into the town proper, for Alice had been determined to have a country house that was accessible to the city. The notion of having the best of both worlds was one that had always appealed to her. "Oh, how lovely!"

"I think it's horrible," said a voice, accompanied by a gentle snore. She turned to see that the caterpillar had sewn himself up in his own clothing and fallen asleep; and the speaker was, this time, the Cheshire Cat, who tipped its head to one side and grinned at her with sharp and feral jaws.

"How can you say that?" she asked it.

"Easy," said the Cat. "I just move my mouth, and words come out." The grin was triumphant. "See, I did it again. Ooh, and again— and again—"

"But the view." She gestured towards it. "It's beautiful, this world of ours— or of mine, rather."

"Selfish," said the Cat, and sniffed.

"Well, it certainly isn't yours. There aren't any Cats that can speak here, or Hares, and for that matter the Hatters are very rarely, if ever, actually mad."

"That's what *you* think," said the Cat.

"It is what I think! I quite realize that you've your own place to get to, and I can't help but wonder why you've all stopped here."

The Cat arose from its position, and stretched impossibly long legs. "Well you may wonder," it said, and yawned. "Well you may wander, as well. You may wonder to wander, and wander to Wonder, and if you wander in Wonder you're almost certain to get lost."

"Lost?" she repeated.

"Almost," admitted the Cat. It sat down beside her and commenced to purr. "As for me, I don't see what's so wonderful about this world of yours. It can't hold a candle to a—"

"To a what?"

"To a candle," said the Cat, leaned over and grinned in her face, eyes shut in sheer ecstasy. "To me, this place is misbegotten, lost on its own terms; an anteroom, a demi-hell, a small landlocked bubble of brine."

"Well, if you don't like it," said Alice, stung, "then rest assured you are welcome to leave."

The Cat's eyes widened. "Am I?" it cried, delighted, and laughed a bit. "Now, *that* is something worth calling wonderful."

It disappeared, and Alice sat quietly on the mushroom top for a moment, thinking to herself and watching her world in front of her; then she walked down the stair-steps again, carefully and deliberately this time, and crossed the lawn to the front door.

The cottage was silent and empty, except for the Hatter,

who'd been waiting for her in the kitchen. She joined him at the table, and smiled at him sadly.

"Tea," said the Hatter promptly, scrambling off his chair to make her some. "Tea is good for depression— or rather, bad for it. At least, that's what they told me at the Sanguinarium." He fumbled the cups athletically down onto the table in front of them, like someone who could do cup-fumbling for England and take home the gold. "It also cures mumps."

"I'm not depressed," said Alice. "I'm merely wondering."

The Hatter slid back into his chair with nonchalance, as though he'd never left it, and nodded deeply. "I can't say I'm surprised— or rather, I could, but I won't, because I am not. That reminds me of a riddle."

"Everything reminds you of a riddle," said Alice, sipping her tea.

"What is it that beats, hops, soars, and stops?" The Hatter wriggled in his chair, pleased with himself, and Alice fell to pondering for a bit.

"Your heart," she replied at last, quite happy that at last he had asked her a question that she could answer.

"Wrong!" cried the Hatter gleefully. "The answer is, a drum, a rabbit, a bird, and a watch. See if I ask *you* anything again." He took a deep swill of his tea and sighed happily. "A Hatter could get used to a thing like this."

Alice smiled at him gently. "Teatime in the kitchen with good companionship?"

"No, china cups," corrected the Hatter, smiling gently back and stirring his tea in dreamy circles with his finger. Alice sat up straight, and sighed.

"When the tea is gone, will you be gone as well?" she asked him softly.

"Quite naturally," said the Hatter, taking another sip. "I only stuck it out for the beverage, anyway."

"Ah, then you agree with the Cat that this is a horrible place?" Alice folded her arms in some displeasure. The Hatter took his time, considering his answer.

"Well, I don't think much of the location," he began at last, glancing out the window, and then he turned a beatific smile on Alice. "But the decor—"

She directed a flushed and flattered smile into her teacup.

"— is absolutely horrible," finished the Hatter, and drained his cup.

She expected him to say, "Well, I must be off—" or, perhaps, "No time like the present—" or at the very least, "Goodbye—" But he said nothing, absolutely nothing, only doffed his hat to her with a deep bow, and strode out the back door and into being gone. She was left alone in the kitchen, and her feet suddenly felt very cold.

It struck her quite abruptly that the scent she'd been inhaling since she returned to the house was the sweetcakes she'd been mixing when this whole escapade began; she opened the oven door to find them completed, done to perfection, in wonderful timing, and that the Hatter had arranged them in suits: hearts, clubs, spades, diamonds. In some delight she fell on a warm heart-shaped sweetcake, to help her finish off her tea, and just before she bit into it she took time to pause.

"I wonder," she asked herself, "if this will make me grow any smaller—?"

She thought about it.

She shook her head. "Now you're just being ridiculous, Alice," she told herself firmly. "You've been grown for years now— as if anything could ever make you smaller, ever again."

She fell to eating, happily.